INTRIGUING
TALE OF CLONING AND BIO-WARFARE

CALL ME c-LUNA

CHANDNI JAFRI

notionpress.com

INDIA • SINGAPORE • MALAYSIA

ISBN

Domestic: 978-93-340-0188-4
International: 979-8-89133-864-7

Contact: business@soundnlight.in for collaboration requests

Table of Contents

Dedication

To my father, Vilayet Jafri.

From the very beginning, you held my hand with a tender touch, guiding me as I clumsily grasped a pencil and scribbled my first hesitant letters. You applauded, even when my words appeared as mere scrawls on the page. You always urged me to find my voice and speak my truth, no matter how uncertain or imperfect. Even though you are not here today, I feel your loving presence guiding me.

Acknowledgements

To all those who have played a part, from the initial spark of inspiration to the final pages, your presence and involvement have made a profound impact, shaping this book into what it has become. Thank you from the bottom of my heart.

Special thanks to Krishna Jafri, Shanaz Sarin, Somit Doshi, Shilpi Srivastava, Jamshed Mistry and Preeta Sinha. This book would not have been possible without your constant guidance, inspiration, and support.

Cloning, Deception, and Genetic Domination

Genetic engineering and animal cloning, often viewed as biotechnological marvels, possess a unique power that grants humans the ability to play a role akin to that of God, sculpting life's intricate forms and functions.

By controlling genetic codes, scientists can design organisms to meet specific criteria, granting them traits or abilities previously unimaginable.

Whoever masters genetic engineering and animal cloning indeed possesses the key to potentially dominating the world. Control over food sources, medicine, and even the development of entirely new life forms could tip the scales of power on a global scale.

In the past few years, scientists from several countries have taken steps to develop cloning technologies for livestock.

However, the immediate commercialization of these technologies remains questionable and controversial due to serious concerns around human and animal health and the potential misuse of the technology for ulterior motives.

Some countries have enforced an outright ban, while others have permitted it with caveats. Investigative reports from the media and other voluntary organisations have revealed that, in spite of the ban, milk and meat from cloned cows are secretly and illegally going into high-street shops and supermarket shelves.

In countries where there is no express ban, independent scientists and think tanks have warned that animal clones are unsuitable for human consumption and that consumers need to be protected from food-borne illnesses resulting from 'unhealthy' clones flooding the food supply.

Critics of this technology argue that a powerful minority of scientists are pushing these technologies simply because they could be lucrative. Science has sold out—particularly in animal agriculture—triggering pandemics, climate change, and bio-warfare.

Call Me c-Luna is a fictional thriller inspired by real-life developments and advancements in genetic engineering and animal cloning.

This work intends to engage and captivate readers with a thrilling storyline, exploring the possibilities of technology, science, and the human-animal connection. In a world where the frontiers of science have pushed humanity to the brink of a new era, Genetic Domination emerges as the clandestine superpower lurking in the shadows, ready to seize command and control.

Will humanity emerge victorious or be forever trapped in its clutches?

Disclaimer: While the story is grounded in scientific plausibility, certain elements and extrapolations may be speculative or fictionalised for the purposes of the narrative.

Prologue

To those who challenge norms and dream,
This book is, for you, an enchanting theme,
"Call Me c-Luna", an intriguing tale,
A journey of courage that will never fail.

In pages adorned with words and ink,
Imagination soars, no limits to think,
With every line, curiosity stirs,
Unveiling truths, where mystery lurks.

For those who believe in compassion's might,
And the harmony between darkness and light,
This book is for you, to ignite the flame,
A reminder of the power we all must claim.

Chapter 1

The Key to Riches

It was a beautiful day.

The NectarMeadow pasture stretched out, a breath-taking expanse of nature's splendour. The vibrant green grass swayed gently in the breeze, creating a mesmerizing wave-like motion that seemed to dance with life. Each blade glistened with dewdrops, catching the sunlight and creating a sparkling mosaic of nature's brilliance.

The air was crisp and clean, carrying the scent of fresh grass and earth. The songs of birds filled the air, their melody harmonizing with the gentle rustling of leaves in nearby trees.

But the beauty of the day was lost on Malcolm, obscured by the storm brewing within his own heart.

Malcolm Thornton, the third-generation NectarMeadow dairy farm owner, sat in his office overlooking the pasture, consumed with worry and deep frustration.

The initial success that propelled him forward and fuelled his desire for more has now turned into an unyielding source of anxiety.

Malcolm froze with fear as his phone rang, the shrill sound cutting through the room's silence. He knew in his gut that this call was the one he had been dreading—the call that would determine the fate of his family's legacy. With trembling hands, he reluctantly answered, bracing himself for the words that would send his world spiralling into chaos.

Caller: Mr. Thornton, I am calling from Greenhorn Financial. This is regarding your outstanding debts.

Malcolm: What's the urgency? I've been trying my best to make the payments.

Caller: Unfortunately, your payments are overdue, and the debts have accumulated significantly. We need to find a solution. One possibility is to consider mortgaging the farm to settle the debts.

Malcolm: Mortgaging the farm? That's a tough decision to make. It has been in my family for generations.

Caller: I understand your attachment, Mr. Thornton, but we need to explore options.

Malcolm: Is there any other way we can work this out?

Caller: I am sorry; we have already made our final offer to you. You need to make the decision fast.

Malcolm: I... I'll try my best. Please give me a little more time. I can't bear to lose everything.

Caller: I'll grant you 24 hours more, but this is the final extension. Make the most of it, Mr. Thornton. Good luck.

The weight of the conversation settled heavily on Malcolm's shoulders, leaving him with a sinking feeling of desperation. Time was slipping through his fingers, and the pressure to save his family's legacy and his own reputation had reached its breaking point.

Malcolm was overcome with a sense of bewilderment and regret. How had he allowed himself to reach the precipice of disaster? It felt like only yesterday that he was the talk of the town, admired by his peers and envied by his competitors.

As he reflected on his journey, he retraced his steps, searching for the defining moments that had led him to this point of no return.

Malcolm's mind drifted back to that fateful day when, at the tender age of 17, his father's untimely death thrust the heavy responsibility of running the farm on his inexperienced shoulders.

His beloved father's death was a monumental loss to him, but he had no time to grieve as the business of the farm now rested squarely on him.

He had to learn the ropes quickly, navigating the complexities of agricultural practices, financial management, and the unpredictable nature of the industry.

It was a steep learning curve, and there were countless moments of self-doubt and exhaustion, but Malcolm persevered. He envisioned his brand dominating the industry, capturing a larger market share, and reaping even greater profits.

His appetite for success knew no bounds, and he set his sights on expanding NectarMeadow Farm's reach beyond the local market. The allure of power and influence enticed him, propelling him to take calculated risks that others deemed too audacious.

The initial profits and recognition he garnered from transforming the family business into a thriving enterprise ignited a flame within Malcolm. The hunger for more success consumed him, driving him to push boundaries and break through limitations. The thrill of taking risks and reaping the rewards became a constant companion on his journey.

However, as the farm reached its peak production capacity, the growth curve flattened, leaving

Malcolm grappling with decreasing profits and mounting debts.

And today, sitting in his office, Malcolm looked like a mere shadow of his former self.

The weight of the mounting challenges had taken its toll on him, leaving him worn and weary. The Midas touch he once possessed seemed to have deserted him, and no matter how hard he tried, he couldn't turn the tide of misfortune. Every decision he made, every strategy he implemented, fell short of their intended mark.

Malcolm paced back and forth in his office, his footsteps echoing the restlessness within him. His eyes scanned the room, searching for a glimmer of hope, but all he saw were shelves filled with files that contained failed attempts and exhausted options.

His fingers clenched and unclenched as he contemplated the harsh reality before him.

He shouted out loud, as if talking to the shadows. "Tell me what to do? There has to be a way. There must be a way!"

His cry for help merged with the darkness, fading into silence. And as he surveyed the room once more, it became clear that his options were exhausted. The room felt suffocating, closing in on him as if reflecting the constraints of his predicament.

A heavy sigh escaped Malcolm's lips, laden with resignation and defeat. He sank into his chair, his body slumping under the weight of his failures. The once-bold entrepreneur now felt like a mere spectator in his own life, powerless to change the course of events.

As the hours ticked by, Malcolm's mind continued to churn, desperately seeking a solution that remained elusive. The room grew darker, shadows stretching across the walls, mirroring the shadows that now engulfed his spirit.

A sudden ping disrupted the silence. Startled, he turned his attention to his computer screen, where a new email notification blinked impatiently. The message was brief but tantalizing, promising a revolutionary solution to his financial woes.

It spoke of a company, shrouded in secrecy, and whispered to possess the key to unlocking unimaginable riches.

Malcolm's curiosity was piqued as he read the anonymous email that had mysteriously landed in his inbox. The message hinted at a secret that could potentially transform his dairy farm and reignite its profitability. Intrigued yet cautious, he decided to dig deeper and explore the possibilities that lay hidden within and clicked on the "Tell me More" button.

In a flash, another email dropped.

Subject: Confidential Meeting: Important Instructions

Dear Malcolm,

The meeting will take place at Grunge Industrial Shed, a discreet venue specially chosen for its confidentiality and minimal foot traffic. Please make sure to arrive within the next 60 minutes.

It is of the utmost importance that you come alone. This meeting should remain strictly confidential, as the matters to be discussed are sensitive and require discretion. We need to ensure that no unauthorized individuals are present during our conversation.

Please take all necessary precautions to maintain the confidentiality of this meeting. Avoid discussing it with anyone else, both within and outside your organization. This includes refraining from sharing any details, such as the location or purpose, with colleagues or acquaintances.

This email will auto-destruct and disappear from your inbox in the next 30 seconds.

See you then.

Warmly, GenED Inc.

Chapter 2

The c-Deal

Malcolm sets out towards the secret location to uncover the truth behind the enigmatic email. He knew that such a sensitive matter required extreme discretion, as the implications could be profound. He didn't want to draw unnecessary attention or risk exposing his vulnerability to his competitors in the cut-throat industry.

Just in time, before his 60 minutes expired, Malcolm found himself in a dimly lit conference room tucked away in the defunct industrial shed. The atmosphere was charged with anticipation as he anxiously waited for his contact to arrive. The sound of muffled footsteps and the faint aroma of freshly brewed coffee filled the air, and suddenly, a figure emerged from the shadows, approaching Malcolm with calculated steps.

It was Dr. Victoria Stein, CEO of GenED, a woman of remarkable presence and an aura of authority. Dr. Victoria exuded an air of charm and charisma that was hard to resist.

Her piercing gaze bore into Malcolm's soul, yet her eyes revealed nothing more than an inscrutable determination.

"Mr. Thornton," Dr. Victoria began, her voice carrying a subtle edge, "I have the solution you seek. A ground-breaking technology that will revolutionize the dairy industry."

Malcolm leaned forward, his eyes locking with hers. "What do you propose?" he inquired, his voice betraying a blend of hope and scepticism.

Dr. Victoria revealed her grand vision—a cloning technology that could create genetically engineered cows capable of tripling milk production. It was a proposition that defied the boundaries of conventional farming and could potentially reshape the dairy landscape.

Malcolm's eyes widened with amazement, and he stammered. "Dr. Victoria, this is...extraordinary. Triple milk production? It's unheard of! How is this even possible?"

Dr. Victoria, smiling confidently, replied "Malcolm, it all comes down to the power of genetic engineering. Through meticulous manipulation of the cow's DNA, we can unlock their full potential, optimizing their milk-producing abilities beyond anything we've ever seen and generate an endless supply of high-yielding clones."

Malcolm, evaluating the prospects, critically said, "And the market potential? If we can truly achieve this level of milk production and an endless supply of clones, imagine the possibilities, Dr. Victoria!"

Dr. Victoria, with eyes gleaming, echoed Malcolm's sentiments. "Precisely, Malcolm. This technology has the potential to catapult us to the forefront of the industry and secure unparalleled profits. The possibilities are boundless."

The ambitious scope of Dr. Victoria's proposal resonated deeply with Malcolm's hunger for success. However, amidst his growing enthusiasm, a sense of caution lingered in the back of his mind. He couldn't ignore the potential controversies and ethical dilemmas that such a venture would undoubtedly entail. The line between scientific advancement and playing God with nature blurred before him, leaving him torn between the allure of prosperity and the implications of tampering with the very essence of life.

Malcolm, with a bit of hesitation, asked. "But what about the ethical considerations?"

"Will there be concerns among consumers about the safety of the cows and the milk they produce?"

Dr. Victoria nodded, understanding the weight of the questions. "Ah, valid concerns indeed. That's why our approach is rooted in rigorous research and diligent testing. Safety is of critical importance to us."

As the conversation drew to a close, Malcolm found himself at a crossroads. He understood that the path ahead would be fraught with challenges, yet the promise of transformation and unprecedented success beckoned him forward. His mind swirled with visions of vast profits and the acclaim that would come with such a monumental breakthrough.

With an air of finality, Malcolm extended his hand to Dr. Victoria, sealing the deal that would forever alter the course of NectarMeadow and his own destiny.

Back at his office, Malcolm, taking a deep breath, steadied his hand as he reached for the phone. With beads of sweat forming on his forehead, Malcolm dialled the familiar number of Greenhorn Financials.

The phone rang impatiently, each second feeling like an eternity.

"This is Malcolm Thornton. I want to discuss my outstanding debts." The representative on the line paused for a moment, recognizing Malcolm's name. "Ah, Mr. Thornton, we were expecting your decision regarding the mortgage. Have you come to a resolution?"

Malcolm hesitated, knowing that time was slipping away. "Yes, I have. I'm calling to inform you that I won't be proceeding with the mortgage. Instead, I have secured a partnership. They will assist me in resolving my financial situation."

There was a brief silence on the other end, followed by a sigh. "Mr. Thornton, we appreciate your update, but the deadline is fast approaching. We need a concrete plan to proceed."

Malcolm's voice trembled slightly as he continued, "I understand the urgency. I'm prepared to make a partial payment today as a sign of my commitment. It won't settle the entire debt, but it's a step towards finding a solution."

The representative on the line was sceptical. "Mr. Thornton, I can't make any promises. We need to evaluate the feasibility of your proposal. Please stay on the line as I discuss this with my superiors."

After a short hold, the representative finally confirmed, "Given the circumstances, we can grant you a brief extension, but only if you provide us with a detailed payment plan."

A wave of relief washed over Malcolm.

The phone call with Greenhorn Financials had bought him some much-needed time. He savoured this fleeting sense of victory. He knew it was a temporary reprieve, but for now, it was enough.

Chapter 3

Trust No One

After sealing the deal with Malcolm, a surge of exhilaration coursed through Dr. Victoria's veins.

With a sense of urgency burning in her eyes, she hurriedly made her way through the dimly lit streets towards the desolate industrial area located 50 kilometres north of her current location. The abandoned shed, nestled among the forgotten remnants of a once-thriving industrial era, served as her makeshift GenED headquarters.

The interior of the industrial shed was dimly lit, with the only source of illumination emanating from a series of flickering fluorescent lights hanging from the ceiling. Dr. Victoria's footsteps echoed against the concrete floor as she navigated through the maze of crates and discarded machinery, her path lit by the faint glow of her smartphone screen. The moment had come to make the all-important call, to solidify her position and execute her grand scheme. She hurried towards her private sanctuary, the camouflaged Video Pod.

As she pressed the concealed button to the Video Pod, she could almost taste the sweet victory within her grasp. With a swift motion, the Pod jutted out of the wall. She activated the door's mechanism, and it slid open soundlessly. The Pod beckoned her; its ultra-tech, high-security design provided a sense of invincibility.

Stepping inside the capsule-shaped Pod, she was enveloped in a cocoon of silence, the heavy door sealing shut behind her, shutting out the world.

The walls, lined with mirrors, reflected her image back at her, each reflection more determined than the last. The mirrored walls captured every angle and every nuance of her expression, amplifying her presence with multiple reflections.

Concealed within the Pod was a sophisticated video booth equipped with state-of-the-art technology. The booth remained hidden until activated with the flick of a switch. As Dr. Victoria flicked the switch, the booth's mechanisms whirred to life. The screen slid open, revealing a high-resolution display and a camera, ready to connect. The mirrored walls surrounding her reflected the screen's glow, amplifying its radiance.

Looking at her multiple reflections in the Pod, she felt an overwhelming sense of control, her voice ready to resonate with calculated impact.

Inhaling sharply, Dr. Victoria positioned herself in front of the booth's screen and adjusted her appearance, ensuring every detail conveyed authority and confidence. With a steady hand, she activated the video call. The screen came alive with the images of the Inner Circle members of the Cloning Confederate.

Dr. Victoria: (smiling) Gentlemen, thank you for gathering here today. I must say, the progress we've made at NectarMeadow has exceeded even my own expectations.

Cloning Confederate Member 1: Excellent news, Dr. Victoria. We're pleased to see your dedication to our cause. The potential of getting an endless supply of cloned animals for bio-warfare and valuable research data is truly promising.

Dr. Victoria: Absolutely. This is just the beginning. Our experiments will pave the way for a revolution in genetic engineering, offering limitless possibilities for the Cloning Confederate.

Cloning Confederate Member 2: We must ensure that our advancements remain under our control, Dr. Victoria. The potential risks associated with this technology leaking out are significant, and we cannot afford any missteps.

Dr. Victoria: Your concerns are valid, and I share your caution. I have implemented strict protocols to safeguard our covert lab, to be set up in a shed at NectarMeadow.

Cloning Confederate Member 1: We trust in your expertise, Dr. Victoria. The success of our organization depends on the breakthroughs you are making. However, we must remain vigilant. Our enemies are watching, and any leaks could jeopardize everything we've built.

Dr. Victoria: Thank you for your trust, gentlemen. I assure you, I will continue to deliver results that exceed your expectations. Together, we will shape the future and fulfil the Cloning Confederate's vision of world-domination.

Switching the screen off, Dr. Victoria swivelled in her chair, thinking to herself how fragile the word "trust" is.

Dr. Victoria trusted no one except the one entity she believed she could rely on completely—herself.

In the confines of her reflective Pod, Dr. Victoria would often stare at her multiple reflections and engage in conversations that only she could hear.

Dr. Victoria: (staring at her reflection in the mirror) You've come so far, Victoria. The Cloning Confederate never saw this coming. Their power, their control... it's time to break free from their clutches.

Mirror Reflection: Bravo, Victoria! Can't believe how the tables have turned. It seems like only yesterday that you were at their mercy without any funding when the government banned your research.

Dr. Victoria: They offered me the funds in lieu of control, but little do they know. I am the one who will seize control. I am nobody's pawn; I am the puppet master.

Mirror Reflection: (smirking) And what will you do, Victoria? What empire will you build in their shadow?

Dr. Victoria: GenED Inc. That's what I'll create. An entity that will surpass everything they've ever imagined. A place where my authority will be absolute and my vision for genetic engineering will shape the future.

Mirror Reflection: But how will you achieve this? NectarMeadow is just the beginning, isn't it?

Dr. Victoria: (grinning) Yes, NectarMeadow is my stepping stone. I sold them on the promise of triple milk production and an endless supply of clones. In exchange, they'll provide the profits I need. And those profits will be my ticket to independence.

Mirror Reflection: Clever, Victoria. But how will you ensure Cloning Confederate don't discover your hidden agenda?

Dr. Victoria: (smiling triumphantly) I've devised a plan. A hidden network of accounts and investments, shielded from their radar. As the profits grow, so will my power. I'll establish my own research facilities, recruit the best scientists, and acquire cutting-edge technology.

Mirror Reflection: Each step forward weakens their grip on you, Victoria. Soon, they'll be nothing more than a memory.

Dr. Victoria: (determined) Yes, they'll fade into insignificance while GenED Inc. rises to prominence. I'll be the one in control, shaping the future of genetic engineering. And they will regret underestimating me.

Mirror Reflection: Embrace your hunger for independence, Victoria. Seize this opportunity and create your empire. The world will bow to your authority.

Dr. Victoria: Oh, they will; yes, they will. The Cloning Confederate will be left behind while I forge my path to dominance. GenED Inc. will be unstoppable.

Reflection: (Dark laughter) Oh, Victoria, in this dance with darkness, remember, I am the only one you can trust.

Dr. Victoria: (Smirking) Undoubtedly. Together, we shall rise, and the world will tremble before us.

Chapter 4

The c-Graves

The following weeks were a whirlwind of activity.

Dr. Victoria and GenED's scientists descended upon NectarMeadow Dairy Farm, their purpose veiled in secrecy. Nestled amongst the sprawling fields, an inconspicuous shed underwent a remarkable transformation. Unbeknownst to the workers and visitors, it became the covert site of a clandestine laboratory.

Inside, rows of sleek workstations housed monitors displaying complex genetic sequences and data, while delicate instruments and vials filled with genetic material covered the lab benches.

Advanced computer terminals blinked with encrypted data, while incubators hummed softly, nurturing the covert creations that would forever alter the course of NectarMeadow's fate.

Within the confines of this facility, rows of cloning chambers stood in eerie silence.

Each chamber housed a delicate and intricate process where the very essence of life was manipulated and replicated.

Dr. Victoria's Video Pod was ingeniously concealed within the heart of her private domain—next to the cloning chambers. It stood as a secret getaway, hidden in plain sight amidst the whirring machinery and pulsating energy of her ingenious experiments.

The process of cloning began with the extraction of genetic material from carefully selected cows known for their high milk yields. This genetic material was then altered using advanced techniques. Dr. Victoria and her team carefully selected and altered specific genes responsible for milk production, aiming to enhance the cows' abilities beyond their natural limits.

Once the genetic modifications were complete, the altered DNA was inserted into emptied cow egg cells. The eggs, now carrying the modified genetic material, were carefully nurtured and triggered to develop into embryos at an accelerated pace.

As the embryos grew, they would be transferred into surrogate cows, who would carry them to term.

These surrogate mothers, unknowing participants in this grand experiment, carried the future of the NectarMeadow project within their wombs.

Their bodies nurtured and sustained the developing clones, each one a genetic masterpiece crafted by the hands of science.

As the experiments continued to progress, Dr. Victoria's mind churned with a sense of urgency and contingency. A crucial juncture had arrived, necessitating an immediate and private meeting with Malcolm.

They retreated to the conference room in the lab. Upon entering the room, Dr. Victoria hastily dimmed the lights, lowered the blinds, and closed the door securely behind her, the click of the latch echoing with finality.

"Malcolm," she began, her voice cold, "there is something I must disclose to you. It pertains to the fate of the surrogate mothers."

Malcolm, sensing the gravity of her words, hunched forward. "What is it, Dr. Victoria? What have we missed?"

Dr. Victoria hesitated; the air felt heavy with the weight of the truth she was about to reveal. "Despite our best efforts, Malcolm, we will not be able to save the surrogate mothers. Their bodies, strained by the size and weight of the cloned calves, will face insurmountable challenges. They will succumb to their postpartum complications. The big challenge here is that we will have to find a way to discreetly dispose of their bodies under the shroud of utmost secrecy."

Malcolm's heart pounded in his chest as Dr. Victoria ended her unsettling revelation. His face turned pale as he struggled to process the horrifying truth about the fate of the surrogate mothers.

"But you assured me when we signed the deal that the procedures would be safe for the cows. Now you're suggesting otherwise?"

Dr. Victoria retorted with a hint of indignation, "Malcolm, progress often comes at a cost. We're pushing the boundaries of science and creating history. The potential benefits of this technology far outweigh the risks. We must accept that there might be some casualties along the way."

Deep down, Malcolm knew that this was not how things were supposed to be. He had envisioned NectarMeadow as a place of business & profits, not a hidden graveyard for innocent lives.

The conflicted emotions overwhelmed him as he looked into Dr. Victoria's eyes. He could see the steely ambition burning within her.

Malcolm understood that he had become entangled in a dangerous web with ramifications far beyond what he had ever imagined.

Silence engulfed the room as Malcolm contemplated his next move. He couldn't simply turn a blind eye to the dark secret that now threatened to taint his farm. He knew that he had to find a way to make things right. But how? The burden of his decision pressed heavily upon him, threatening to suffocate his conscience.

Finally, Malcolm broke the silence. "Dr. Victoria, I can't deny the enormity of what you've just revealed," he began, his voice shaky. "But I refuse to accept that we have no other choice but to dispose of these innocent lives in secret. There must be another way."

Dr. Victoria's eyes narrowed, clearly taken aback by Malcolm's unexpected resistance. "And what, pray tell, do you suggest we do, Malcolm?" She asked, her voice laced with frustration.

"Sentimentality won't change the fact that we have a problem on our hands," she retaliated. "But if it eases your conscience, I suppose we can consider if you have any other suggestions. However, remember that time is of the essence. We cannot afford any disruptions to our plans."

Malcolm nodded, acknowledging the urgency of the situation. He knew that he had to act swiftly to protect the integrity of NectarMeadow and the lives entangled within its walls. His stomach churned with anxiety as he battled with the grim reality before him.

The writing was on the wall, and he came to the sobering realization that there was really no easy way out of the situation he found himself in. The secret burial ground seemed to be the only viable option.

Reluctantly, Malcolm accepted the daunting task that lay ahead. He knew the risks involved, both ethically and legally, but he couldn't possibly dispose of the bio-medical waste and bodies of the surrogates via regular incinerators without arousing suspicion from the authorities and exposing his undercover lab.

With a heavy heart, Malcolm began formulating a plan to execute the secret burials. He recruited a small team of trusted employees, individuals who had shown steadfast loyalty to NectarMeadow over the years. In supreme secrecy, they designated a secluded corner of the property as the final resting place for the surrogate mothers.

After making sure that Malcolm was going to comply, Dr. Victoria made her way to the Cloning Chambers.

She pressed the concealed button and entered her fortress – the Video Pod. It was time for the dialogue.

Dr. Victoria stood before the mirrored walls of her Video Pod, her reflection distorted by the menacing shadows cast upon her face.

Mirror Reflection: (Chuckling darkly) Ah, Victoria, you cunning manipulator. How clever of you to withhold those little details from dear Malcolm! The lure of power blinds him to the truth, doesn't it? The risks, the dangers lurking beneath the surface of your grand design.

Dr. Victoria: (Her expression a mix of satisfaction and deceit) Malcolm's hunger for success and his desperate need for validation make him the perfect pawn. Knowledge is power, and information selectively shared is a potent weapon of control. Why burden him with the truth when I can guide him along?

Mirror Reflection: (Whispering with a sinister tone) Oh, so that's why you still haven't told him about the possibility of clones with organ failures? And what of the unsuspecting souls who consume the tainted milk, unaware of the potential harm it may bring?

Dr. Victoria: (A sinister grin playing upon her lips) The path to power is paved with deception, my dear. And as I lead Malcolm further into the depths of my grand scheme, his ignorance will be my greatest weapon. He will serve me, unknowingly, until the very end.

Mirror Reflection: (eyes gleaming with wicked delight) Ah, the arrogance of a god, willing to play with lives as if they were mere toys. Do you truly believe that your desires outweigh the potential devastation you may unleash upon this world?

Dr. Victoria: (Her gaze hardening) These are necessary risks, calculated gambles in the pursuit of scientific breakthroughs that will shape the future. The world may recoil, but in time, they will come to see the brilliance of my work.

Chapter 5

Embracing the Unknown

As Emma walked through the serene grounds of NectarMeadow farm, she couldn't shake off a sense of unease. The farm, with its lush green pastures and idyllic setting, seemed an unlikely place for a pioneering scientific laboratory.

Nestled within the rustic charm of the farm, the GenED lab felt out of place, almost clandestine.

The lab itself was discreetly tucked away in a secluded corner of the property, shielded from prying eyes. The contrast between the peaceful exterior of the farm and the cutting-edge technology housed within the lab was unsettling to Emma. It was as if two worlds coexisted, one of nature's beauty and the other of scientific experimentation.

As Emma stepped into the GenED laboratory, her veins throbbed with excitement mingled with nervousness. She had dreamed of this moment for years, finally landing a position as a research associate at one of the most prestigious biotech companies.

Today marked the beginning of her journey into the world of radical scientific exploration.

Dr. Victoria Stein, the renowned scientist and CEO of GenED, approached Emma with a warm smile. "Welcome to GenED, Emma Smith," Dr. Victoria greeted her, extending a hand. "I've heard great things about your work, and I'm thrilled to have you as part of our team. We're at the forefront of genetic research, exploring ground-breaking possibilities that will shape the future."

Emma felt flustered, her eyes filled with awe.

Dr. Victoria was renowned for her brilliance in the field, relentless pursuit of innovation, and tenacious dedication to scientific progress. Emma had long admired Dr. Victoria's work, and now standing before her and being personally welcomed was beyond her wildest dreams.

"I'm honoured to be here, Dr. Victoria," Emma replied, her voice filled with genuine enthusiasm. "Your research has been an inspiration to me, and I'm eager to contribute to the advancements being made at GenED."

Dr. Victoria nodded approvingly. "I believe you have the potential to make significant contributions to our projects. We're on the brink of something extraordinary, Emma."

"Together, we will explore the frontiers of genetic engineering and revolutionize the world of science. Do join us in the conference room for an induction into the security protocols required here."

Dr. Victoria Stein gathered the research team in the secluded conference room, her expression serious and commanding. "Team, I cannot stress enough the need for inviolable secrecy in our work here at GenED," Dr. Victoria began, her voice low but firm. "The nature of our research is disruptive, and with it comes great responsibility. The knowledge we possess has the potential to reshape industries, challenge boundaries, and impact the world."

Emma listened intently, but a flicker of confusion crossed her face. She wondered why such elaborate security measures were necessary. After all, they were conducting scientific research, not engaging in espionage.

Dr. Victoria seemed to sense Emma's hesitation and paused, her gaze piercing through the room. "Emma, I understand your confusion, but let me assure you, there are forces at play that would stop at nothing to gain access to our work and exploit it for their own gains. The implications of what we're doing go far beyond the confines of this laboratory."

Emma slowly began to comprehend the gravity of the situation.

The realization that their work held such significant implications and potential consequences had a huge impact on her.

Dr. Victoria's voice softened as she spoke, her expression reflecting firmness. "That is why we must maintain the highest level of discretion and confidentiality. We have implemented stringent security protocols to protect our work, our team, and the integrity of our research. Our commitment to secrecy is not just a matter of professional responsibility but also a matter of personal safety." Allowing a few seconds to let the gravity of her words sink in, Dr. Victoria continued. "The unusual location was a strategic choice. The remote setting offered seclusion and limited access, reducing the chances of unauthorized interference. The farm's operations served as a clever disguise, shielding the lab's true purpose from casual observers."

As the meeting concluded, Dr. Victoria approached Emma, her eyes filled with caution.

Dr. Victoria: Emma, I know this might seem overwhelming, but in time, you will see that the elaborate security measures are not just for show, but a necessary safeguard against external threats.

Emma: (Nodding) I understand, Dr. Victoria. The gravity of our work and the need for secrecy have become clear to me. I am fully committed to upholding confidentiality and protecting the integrity of our mission.

Dr. Victoria: Good to hear that, Emma.

Emma: Thank you, Dr. Victoria. Your trust in me is not taken lightly.

As the day waned into the late hours of the night, Emma found herself seated around a table with her fellow team members. The room was dimly lit, with the soft glow of computer screens casting an ethereal light upon their faces. Fatigue tugged at their weary eyes, but a shared sense of excitement and accomplishment filled the air.

Team members eagerly shared their findings, their voices intermingling with enthusiasm and exhaustion. Charts, graphs, and data filled the room as they dissected the intricacies of their research. Emma listened intently, absorbing every detail, and her mind buzzed with new knowledge.

In spite of the late hour, there was a palpable energy in the room. The camaraderie among the team members was infectious. They exchanged ideas, challenged assumptions, and celebrated breakthroughs, each contribution adding another piece to the puzzle they were collectively unravelling.

As the meeting drew to a close, Emma felt a sense of satisfaction wash over her. She had immersed herself in the world of GenED, absorbing as much information as she could on her first day.

The dedication and passion of her colleagues fuelled her own determination, igniting a fire within her to contribute to the project's success.

With a tired but contented smile, Emma bid her teammates goodnight. She walked out of the lab, the cool night air rejuvenating her weary body. The stars above twinkled, a reminder of the vast possibilities that lay ahead.

Emma knew she had embarked on a thrilling journey that would test her limits, broaden her horizons, and shape her destiny.

Chapter 6

The Silent Cry

The sun was shining brightly on the green pastures of NectarMeadow Dairy Farm, but there was no warmth in Malcolm's heart as he watched the cows graze. The guilt consumed him, a constant reminder of the dark secret he harboured.

The morning was filled with the sweet scent of freshly cut grass. Malcolm stood at the edge of the pasture, his hands tightening the grip on the railing, as he remembered the fateful day when he made the deal with GenED.

His breathing was shallow as his mind filled with the memories of that decisive meeting with Dr. Victoria Stein. Her sleek black suit and confident demeanour had initially captivated him, but now he saw through the polished façade. Her charisma and disarming smile had drawn him into a dangerous dance, seducing him with promises of unimaginable success and wealth.

But now doubt gnawed at his conscience like a relentless predator.

It seemed like the price he was going to pay for success was far greater than he had ever imagined.

He looked at the herd before him, their bodies marked with the tell-tale signs of invasive procedures.

The cows seemed oblivious to his internal struggle, their large eyes half closed, as they grazed the grass with a serene calmness. Malcolm had once believed that their contentment was a sign of their satisfaction, but now he couldn't help but wonder if it was simply their generosity to forgive everything.

Malcolm leaned against the fence, his eyes fixed on Shanti, the gentle cow grazing in the distance who had been selected as a surrogate and was to be shifted to the lab shortly. Aster, the young and vibrant farmhand, was tending to her. Aster and his ancestors had lived and served on the farm for nearly three generations.

Seeing Malcom, Aster rushed to greet him. With fervour and a sparkle in his eyes, he exclaimed "How do you do, Mr. Malcolm? It's a beautiful day, isn't it?

Malcolm nodded, a faint smile touching his lips. "Indeed, Aster. It's hard to deny the charm of this place."

Aster's gaze shifted towards Shanti, his voice filled with admiration and longing.

"You know, Mr. Malcolm, Shanti is one extraordinary cow. She's got this grace and this aura around her that's hard to resist."

Malcolm's smile deepened, and he turned his attention to Aster. "I can see the way you look at her, Aster. She's captured your heart, hasn't she?"

Aster's cheeks flushed, his enthusiasm bubbling over. "Yes, Mr. Malcolm. I can't help but be drawn to her. She's more than just a cow to me. She's like a companion, a friend."

Malcolm's expression softened as he watched the young farmhand. "Aster, I understand your feelings. There's a certain connection we can have with these animals, a bond that goes beyond words."

Aster nodded, his eyes shining with affection. "But sometimes, Mr. Malcolm, I wonder if there's more we can do for them. They give us so much, and yet we still take from them. Shouldn't we give something back?"

Malcolm's eyes met Aster's, and his gaze fused with gratitude and regret. "You're wise beyond your years, Aster."

Malcolm found himself caught in a web of conflicting emotions as he saw Aster's infectious smile and heard love in his voice. He wondered how Aster would react upon learning of the fate of Shanti and how his heart would break.

Yet Malcolm knew that he couldn't delay the inevitable any longer. It was a conversation he both dreaded and longed for, as he yearned for understanding and acceptance from Aster.

As he mustered his resolve, Malcolm reminded himself of the greater purpose that fuelled his actions. The desire to protect the farm was his only true legacy. It was a sacrifice he believed necessary, though it tore at his heart to know the price Shanti would pay.

With a heavy sigh, Malcolm spoke, his voice laced with sorrow and regret. "Aster, I am sorry; there is no easy way to say this. Shanti has been selected as a surrogate, and she will be leaving shortly for the lab." His words hung in the air, silence enveloping them as Aster processed the unexpected news.

Shock and disbelief coursed through Aster. He struggled to find the right words, his voice barely a whisper as he asked, "Why? Why can't Shanti stay here with us?"

Muttering incoherently, Malcolm tried to explain the purpose behind Shanti's departure and the role she was destined to play in the experiments at the lab. But his words fell on deaf ears as Aster's eyes filled with tears of pain and anguish.

"I don't understand," Aster choked out, his voice quivering with emotion. "Shanti belongs here, not in the lab. She is family to me. How can you let them take her away?"

The pain in Aster's words struck a chord within Malcolm, a reminder of the sacrifices they were all making in the name of progress.

Malcolm reached out, placing a comforting hand on Aster's shuddering shoulder. "I never wanted this for Shanti or for us, Aster. But sometimes we have to make difficult choices for the greater good. We have to trust that there's a purpose to it all. I understand if you're angry, Aster. And I can't promise to make everything right. But I need you to understand that this decision was never made lightly. I care for Shanti just as much as you do, and it breaks my heart to see her go. But there's something bigger at stake here, something we may not fully comprehend yet."

Aster averted his gaze, emotions flickering across his face. He wrestled with conflicting feelings of anger, betrayal, and a glimmer of understanding.

With a heavy heart, Malcolm reached out, pulling Aster into a bittersweet embrace.

Malcolm then crossed over the fence to move closer to Shanti. He reached out to stroke Shanti's velvety fur. Her large, vulnerable, and trusting eyes lingered lovingly on Malcolm.

"I'm sorry," he whispered, his voice barely a breath. "I didn't know. I didn't understand."

Shanti nuzzled against his hand, her gentle touch offering a flicker of solace amidst the overwhelming guilt. It felt like a silent reassurance, a heart-rending comfort. At that moment, Malcolm convinced himself that he was making the right choice and that his decision to proceed with Dr. Victoria's plan was driven by necessity, not greed.

Abruptly, Malcolm turned away from the herd and headed back towards his office. As he entered his office, he hastily moved towards the window overlooking the pasture. With a sharp tug, he yanked the blinds down, hoping to block out the torment in his heart. His eyes turned towards the family portrait hanging on the wall. It was a precious heirloom, a testament to the legacy of proud dairy farmers that his father and grandfather had upheld. In the dim light of the office, the portrait seemed to come alive, their eyes peering into his soul, questioning his every decision.

"I hope you understand," Malcolm whispered. "I'm doing what I think is best."

The dance with the shadows had begun, and Malcolm knew that he would have to confront the darkness within himself. The question that lingered, haunting his thoughts, was whether he would emerge from this dance unscathed or forever trapped in its clutches.

Chapter 7

The Borderline

From the moment Emma stepped foot into the GenED lab, she knew she had to prove herself. With each passing day, Emma's skills sharpened, her intellect shining brightly. She immersed herself in her work, earning the respect and admiration of her team members.

Dr. Victoria had been observing Emma's progress with keen interest, her dedication and remarkable contributions not going unnoticed. As the Surrogacy Program gained momentum, it became evident to Dr. Victoria that Emma possessed the unique combination of skills and insight necessary to lead the team to new heights.

One day, in a private meeting, Dr. Victoria sat down with Emma and shared her decision. The words fell on Emma's ears like a symphony of surprise and honour. She was being promoted to the coveted position of Program Lead for the Surrogacy Program.

Emma's heart fluttered with a mix of elation and trepidation.

She felt an overwhelming sense of gratitude for the recognition of her hard work and dedication.

However, a flicker of doubt surfaced within her. Did she truly deserve this position? She couldn't help but think of Fred, her senior colleague, who had poured months of research and expertise into the program. Without a doubt, Fred was far more deserving than her.

She began to speak tentatively. "Dr. Victoria, I appreciate your confidence in me, but I must admit, I'm feeling a bit overwhelmed by this proposition. It's a tremendous responsibility, and I'm not sure if I'm ready for it."

Dr. Victoria: Emma, I understand your hesitation, and it's natural to feel overwhelmed when presented with such an opportunity. But let me assure you, I see something special in you. Your dedication, passion, and unique perspective make you the perfect person to lead the Surrogacy Program into a new era.

Emma: But I'm still learning, Dr. Victoria. There's so much I don't know, and the weight of this responsibility feels immense.

Dr. Victoria: That's precisely why I believe in you, Emma. Your fresh ideas and unique perspective will add a new dimension to our work. You have the ability to inspire the team and ignite their creativity and passion.

Emma: I appreciate your faith in me, Dr. Victoria. It means a lot. But what if I make mistakes? What if I can't live up to the expectations?

Dr. Victoria: Emma, mistakes are a part of growth and learning. We all make them. What matters is how we respond to and learn from them. I have confidence in your abilities.

Emma: I never expected to be given such an opportunity, Dr. Victoria. It's both exhilarating and terrifying at the same time. But I'm willing to step up, to embrace this challenge, and to contribute in any way I can.

Dr. Victoria: That's the spirit, Emma. Embrace the exhilaration; embrace the unknown.

Emma: Thank you, Dr. Victoria. Your belief in me means a lot. I'm ready to take on this responsibility.

Dr. Victoria: Good call. Congratulations! Let me announce this to the team right away.

Dr. Victoria gathered the team in the conference room, her eyes gleaming with foretaste. She announced, "Today, we embark on a significant milestone in our Surrogacy Program. I am very happy to announce that Emma Smith has been appointed as the head of the Surrogacy Program"

As the team members congratulated Emma, there were some unspoken words etched on their faces. Some questioned the decision, wondering if she was truly prepared for the challenges ahead.

Others saw her appointment as a breath of fresh air, a chance to inject new perspectives into the Program.

Dr. Victoria continued, "Emma, your first assignment will be to conduct a comprehensive medical profile on Shanti, our first surrogate candidate. You need to assess Shanti's medical readiness for the embryo implant. Embryo implantation in Shanti is our pilot project. And once this succeeds, we will replicate this in 100 more surrogates. Please get going immediately." And with that, Dr. Victoria walked out of the room.

As the team dispersed, Emma found herself drawn to the window overlooking the pasture, where Shanti grazed peacefully. The golden hues of the setting sun bathed the landscape, casting a warm glow upon her. Emma marvelled at the natural beauty and inherent dignity and grace Shanti exuded.

Emma's mind grappled with conflicting emotions. On the one hand, she understood the significance of this moment for scientific progress. On the other hand, she felt a deep sense of empathy and connection to Shanti, making the prospect of confining her and subjecting her to laboratory procedures all the more difficult to bear.

Drawing in a breath, Emma approached Shanti's medical file, brimming with data and test results. Each page held a piece of the cow's story, with her genetic makeup and health history systematically documented. Emma's hands trembled slightly as she flipped through the pages; a rush of emotions built up within her.

Emma marvelled at the cow's resilience and the delicate intricacies of her physiology.

With each piece of information uncovered, Emma's compassion for Shanti deepened.

With her heart and mind aligned, Emma was ready to face the challenges that lay ahead. She hurried out of the lab, looking forward to getting home for her well-earned sleep.

As Emma stepped out of the lab, the air around her seemed charged with tension. A flickering streetlamp cast long shadows, amplifying the turmoil she felt within herself. It was then that she noticed a figure lurking in the darkness.

The silhouette emerged from the shadows, revealing itself to be Aster, his face etched with anguish. His eyes gleamed with fear and desperation as he confronted Emma with an intensity that sent shivers down her spine.

"Shanti... she can't be taken away," Aster's sad voice was defiant. "I'll do anything to keep her here, to protect her. She's everything to me."

Caught off guard by Aster's sudden outburst, Emma struggled to find the right words, torn between the duty entrusted to her and the depth of Aster's emotions.

She could see the anguish etched on his face—the raw pain of separation from a companion who had become a cherished part of his life.

"Aster, I hear your plea, and I understand your love for Shanti," Emma said, her voice steady but filled with compassion. "I promise you that once the calf is born, Shanti will come back to you. She will be reunited with you, and you will have the opportunity to continue the life you share."

Aster's eyes welled up with hope, but disbelief tugged at him. His shivering hands reached out to grasp Emma's, as if seeking reassurance that this promise was indeed real.

Emma's heart ached as she looked into Aster's eyes, witnessing the profound connection he shared with Shanti.

She spoke softly, "I promise. Please go back now, Aster."

With tears in his eyes, as Aster turned to leave, he said, "I will be waiting for her." And slowly, he retreated into the shadows.

The sharp ring of the phone pierced through the stillness of the night, jolting Malcolm awake from a restless sleep. Disoriented, he fumbled for the receiver, his voice groggy as he answered.

"Malcolm, it's Victoria," came the searing voice at the other end, devoid of any trace of sleep. Malcolm's mind felt foggy as he glanced at the clock, the glowing digits reading 3:00 am.

"Dr. Victoria, it's the middle of the night," Malcolm protested, his voice laced with weariness. "Can't this wait until morning?"

For a moment, Malcolm thought he had managed to dissuade her. But then, Dr. Victoria's voice turned cold and unforgiving, her tone laced with authority.

"Malcolm, I demand that you take immediate action," she commanded, her words cutting through the air like a sharp blade. "Our security cameras caught Aster trespassing."

"Aster's presence at the farm poses a threat to our operations. He must be removed, effective immediately."

"Dr. Victoria, you have to understand," Malcolm pleaded, his voice tinged with desperation.

"Aster has been a loyal and hardworking member of the team. He cares deeply for the cows, especially Shanti. Dismissing him would devastate him."

There was a pause at the other end of the line, and Malcolm held his breath, hoping that his words had made some sense to Dr. Victoria. Finally, her voice softened ever so slightly, a hint of contemplation seeping through the cracks.

"Malcolm, I know this is difficult, but we must prioritize the success of our project," Dr. Victoria reasoned. "Aster's emotional attachment compromises our security and undermines the confidentiality we have worked so hard to maintain."

"Fine." Malcolm acquiesced, his voice filled with resignation. "I'll handle it."

"Very well." Her voice was softer than before. "But make it quick. We cannot afford any disruptions or leaks. I want you to ensure that from tomorrow onwards there is no trespassing from NectarMeadow into the GenED lab," she stated firmly.

"Why the sudden overreaction, Dr. Victoria?" Malcolm questioned, his voice laced with curiosity and a touch of suspicion.

"We've always upheld the separation between NectarMeadow and the lab."

Dr. Victoria's response came swiftly, her words carrying an undercurrent of urgency. "Recent developments have necessitated heightened security measures. We cannot afford any breaches of confidentiality or interference with our research.

The work we are undertaking is delicate, and we must protect it at all costs."

Malcolm's response came hesitantly. "I... I'll do my best to reinforce the security protocols," he stammered, his uncertainty seeping through his words.

Dr. Victoria: "Good. Make sure that no one from NectarMeadow crosses over to GenED without proper authorization from me."

Chapter 8

Uneasy Love

As Emma entered the lab the next day, an uneasy feeling settled in the pit of her stomach. Something was off, and she felt a growing sense of discomfort that coursed through her veins.

The once-familiar atmosphere of camaraderie and collaboration now felt stifled and suffocated by the tightened security measures.

Emma's footsteps echoed through the corridor as she made her way towards her workstation. The usual buzz of conversation had been replaced by hushed whispers and cautious glances. The once vibrant and lively lab now felt like an inaccessible fortress, where trust had given way to an atmosphere of caution.

As she sat down, Emma felt a sharp pang of uncertainty. The change in security protocol has cast a shadow over the once-thriving research environment. It was as if a veil had been drawn over the lab, separating it not only from the outside world but also isolating those within its walls.

As the day progressed, Emma's discomfort grew. Each surveillance camera and each restricted access door only served to deepen her sense of restlessness. She felt that she was being watched, her every move scrutinized.

Emma's heart raced as she approached the heavily guarded Surrogate Enclosures; their stark resemblance to a fortified prison stirred up a queasy feeling. The air crackled with unsettling energy, suffocating her with a sense of confinement and surveillance.

As Emma neared the entrance, the heavy metal door seemed like an unyielding barrier. With wobbly hands, she reached for the access card. The metallic click of the gate unlocking reverberated in the silence, a foreboding reminder of the controlled environment she was about to step into.

Inside, the enclosure felt like a sterile prison, devoid of the warmth and tranquillity that should have accompanied Shanti's presence. Cold, stainless steel fences lined the boundaries, their harsh lines enclosing the space with clinical precision.

Emma's gaze fell on Shanti, her heart sinking at the sight.

The majestic creature stood confined, her noble spirit diminished within the boundaries of this artificial prison. Shanti's eyes, once filled with a sense of freedom, now mirrored a yearning for the vast expanse that lay beyond those imposing walls.

With gentle, reassuring whispers, Emma approached Shanti, her hands quivering as she prepared to take the necessary samples. She wanted to make sure that she did not intrude upon Shanti's sense of autonomy.

Kneeling beside Shanti, she stroked her sleek coat and spoke in hushed tones, her voice a soothing melody in the sterile surroundings.

Slowly, Emma began the process. She collected hair samples, taking care not to cause any discomfort to Shanti. As she carefully extracted blood samples, Emma maintained a delicate balance between efficiency and tenderness. With each needle prick, she murmured soothing words, her voice carrying a sense of understanding and gratitude for Shanti's cooperation.

She sought to foster a connection, to assure Shanti that she was not alone in this sterile world.

Emma's touch was feather-light as she swabbed Shanti's skin, capturing genetic material that would be analysed with great precision. She kept her movements slow and deliberate, ensuring that Shanti felt safe and respected throughout the process.

Her heart ached for this magnificent being, and she longed for the day when Shanti would be free once more.

Emma whispered the dream of a future to Shanti where her offspring would flourish and roam free in the fields of NectarMeadow, basking in the warm sun.

With a resolute spirit, Emma turned away, carrying the weight of Shanti's story and the countless others who would be joining the Surrogacy Program.

As Emma entered the lab, her mind felt muddled. She sought validation and guidance from Fred, her trusted senior colleague, hoping he could shed light on the unsettling events taking place.

"Fred, do you have a moment?" Emma approached him, her voice tinged with concern.

Fred, who had been engrossed in his work, looked up and gave a half-hearted smile. "Sure, Emma. What's on your mind?"

Emma carefully chose her words. "I've noticed some unusual things happening here, Fred. The heightened security and secrecy surrounding the project are making me very uneasy. Have you noticed anything strange?"

Fred's eyes shifted nervously, his manner suddenly guarded. "I'm not sure what you're talking about, Emma. Everything seems in order to me."

Emma was crestfallen, a wave of dejection washing over her. It was as if their camaraderie had evaporated, replaced by a wall of indifference. "Fred, we used to be a team. I thought we could trust each other. But it feels like something has changed."

Fred's eyes briefly met hers, filled with guilt and unease. "Look, Emma, I...I have my own reasons for staying out of all this. It's nothing personal. I just need to focus on my work."

Emma's disappointment transformed into frustration. "So, now that I'm supposed to be your so-called 'boss', do we stop being the team we used to be? Is that it, Fred?"

Fred squirmed in his seat, avoiding her gaze. "It's not like that, Emma. I just have my own priorities and deliverables that I need to stay focused on."

Emma felt a sense of despair, realising that their once strong bond had weakened. "I understand, Fred. We all have our priorities. I just thought we could count on each other, especially in times like these."

Fred's expression softened momentarily, and a hint of regret flickered in his eyes. "I'm sorry, Emma. I didn't mean to let you down. It's just... complicated."

Emma nodded, disappointment and resignation filling her heart. "I get it, Fred. We all have our battles to fight. Just know that I'm here, trying to do what's right. I hope you'll reconsider and stand with me when the time comes."

As Emma made her way back to her desk, she forced herself to push aside her disappointment and focus on the tasks at hand. Tomorrow was a crucial day—the embryo implant for Shanti. If all the reports come back positive, it would mark a significant milestone in the project.

She knew that in the next two days, she would need the cooperation and support of her entire team. With so much at stake, she couldn't let Fred's evasiveness deter her.

Emma delved into her work, thoroughly reviewing the medical profiles, double-checking the lab reports, and ensuring that everything was in order for the upcoming procedure. Once the embryo was implanted, she hoped to have a clearer understanding of the project's direction and the motives behind the heightened security measures. It was then, after the implant, that she planned to have another conversation with Fred.

Wrapping up her day, Emma walked into the night. It felt like the night held a stillness that matched her weary soul.

As Emma lay in her bed, sleep eluded her as her heart spoke a revelation she had been hesitant to acknowledge.

It was more than just a feeling of camaraderie that she felt for Fred.

She had felt drawn to Fred's warmth, wisdom, and gentle guidance right from her early days at the lab. Fred had taken her under his wing, helping her learn the ropes.

Emma realised that her admiration for Fred had blossomed into something more.

Was it love?

Perhaps, but they will never know. With the new dynamics at work, she felt that their connection could get stifled, maybe even shattered. She wondered if Fred's evasiveness was a deliberate attempt to keep their relationship strictly professional. Perhaps he too had sensed the shifting dynamics and wanted to preserve their friendship, knowing the risks of diving into something deeper.

The realization left Emma feeling vulnerable and unsure of how to proceed. She yearned for the simplicity of the earlier days, when their interactions were unburdened by the weight of authority.

Now, the boundaries between their personal and professional lives seemed impenetrable, trapping her feelings within the confines of her heart.

The night stretched on, and Emma grappled with the conflicting desires that battled within her.

She understood the importance of maintaining professionalism and focusing on their work, but her heart longed for something more—a connection that transcended the boundaries of their roles.

With newfound courage, Emma decided to have an open conversation with Fred, revealing her true emotions and feelings.

In the hushed embrace of the night, she whispered a silent plea to the universe, "May love find its way," her words drifting into the vastness of the night sky.

Chapter 9

Secrets and Shadows

The ring jolted Emma awoke, scattering the remnants of her restless slumber. She fumbled to pick up the phone, feeling a rush of adrenaline. It was the call she had been anxiously awaiting—the confirmation that the tests for Shanti had come back positive.

"Emma, it's the technician," the voice on the other end crackled with urgency. "The results are in. Shanti is ready for the implantation. Everything looks promising." Emma felt an upsurge of excitement in her being. The big day had arrived.

With a newfound energy, Emma leaped out of bed, her mind already racing with plans and preparations. She hastily dressed, the magnitude of the day propelling her forward.

As she dashed through the early morning streets, the city still slumbering in darkness, Emma's thoughts coalesced into a singular focus to make the procedure a grand success.

The lab doors swung open, and Emma entered with a purpose, her steps steadfast and her mind razor sharp. The team buzzed around her, sensing the gravity of the day ahead.

And there he was, Fred, standing at his workstation with a warm smile that sent a throb of excitement coursing through her being. Her heart skipped a beat as their eyes met, the connection between them palpable and electrifying.

Fred's smile widened as Emma approached. "Good morning, Emma," he greeted her, his voice filled with familiarity and newfound tenderness. The sound of her name on his lips stirred something deep within her, igniting a cascade of emotions she couldn't deny.

"Good morning," Emma replied, her voice infused with delight and a bit of nervousness. As they stood face-to-face, a subtle undercurrent circulated in the air, a silent invitation to explore the uncharted space of their emotions. In that fleeting moment, the world around them faded into the background, leaving only the presence of each other and the magnetic pull drawing them closer.

Just as Emma and Fred were immersed in the unspoken energy between them, they were abruptly interrupted by the urgent voice of the lab technician.

"Emma, Fred, we need you both in the operating room. Shanti is ready for the next stage."

The doors to the operating room swung open, revealing Shanti strapped up with multiple monitoring devices and surrounded by a carefully arranged array of medical equipment. As Dr. Victoria's face flickered on the large video screen, the room fell into a hushed silence as her voice resonated through the speakers. "All set, team? Emma, go on, take the lead."

Emma donned her surgical gown and gloves, her eyes fixed on the delicate instruments before her. She listened intently as Dr. Victoria's voice echoed in her ears.

Shanti's breath rose and fell in a rhythmic cadence, her trust placed in the hands of the team before her. She was a vessel of hope, a living testament to the possibilities of science.

Gently, Emma picked up the carefully prepared vial containing the cloned embryo, its contents shimmering with the promise of a new life. The room held its breath as she approached Shanti's side, her hands stable and sure. The implantation process began—a dance of delicate precision and unflinching focus. Emma's hands moved with expertise, and as the embryo found its place within Shanti's womb, the procedure reached a successful close.

A collective sense of relief washed over the room.

Dr. Victoria's voice boomed through the room: "Congratulations, Emma and team! Well done!"

Through the layers of masks, smiles were shared, and nods of agreement acknowledged the excitement of the achievement as the team began exiting the operating room. Emma's gaze gravitated towards Fred. In the middle of the contagious jubilation, she detected a subtle disquiet in his eyes—a flicker of anxiety and a hint of sadness that contrasted with the exuberance surrounding them.

Just as Emma and Fred exited, a momentary collision between them caused Emma's papers to flutter through the dimly lit corridor. Emma's files were scattered across the floor, mingling with the shadows cast by flickering lights.

In that split second, Fred instinctively bent down, his hand reaching out to assist Emma in gathering the scattered papers. Their eyes met briefly, and Fred's voice barely above a whisper murmured to Emma, "I've slipped a note. Read it in private. Destroy after reading."

As the echoes of Fred's whispered message reverberated in her mind, Emma took a deep breath, steadying herself against the flood of emotions that threatened to overwhelm her.

With tentative steps, she made her way through the bustling corridor to the nearby Ladies Room.

Emma locked herself in one of the stalls, carefully unfolded the piece of paper, and scanned the note. The message was cryptic yet compelling. It read, "Meet me at Proto restaurant in town. 8 PM tonight. Do not mention this meeting to anyone. Destroy after reading."

Emma's breath caught in her throat as she felt flooded with excitement. As she began shredding the note, she felt a faint undercurrent of apprehension building up. What could Fred possibly want to discuss in such secrecy?

She dropped the shredded pieces of the note into the toilet bowl and watched as they vanished beneath the swirling water.

As she made her way back to her desk, her mind flared up with questions. Emma felt overwhelmed, but she tried to force herself to remain composed and to play her part amidst the watchful eyes of their colleagues and invading security cameras. The day's events, the operation's success, the unspoken bond she shared with Fred, and now this cryptic note seemed to intertwine, fuelling a fire within her.

Emma nervously glanced at her wrist, her gaze fixated on the ticking digits of her watch.

Time seemed to slow down as each passing second felt like an eternity. Her thoughts raced, her imagination painting vivid pictures of what might transpire.

Emma's pulse quickened as the clock struck 7pm. She hurriedly finished her tasks, her mind preoccupied with the approaching meeting.

As Emma made her way towards the busy restaurant, her heart thumped with expectation. In that fleeting second, Emma sensed that her life was about to take an unexpected turn in a way she could never have foreseen.

Chapter 10

The Secret Rendezvous

Emma's footsteps faltered as she stepped into the bustling restaurant, the cacophony of voices crashing against her senses. She felt a tinge of doubt creeping in. The blaring sounds of chatter and clinking glasses clashed with the image of a quiet, intimate conversation she had envisioned.

The realisation hit her like a wave—this was not the romantic setting she had imagined for a first date. This place was worlds away from the intimacy she craved.

Had she misinterpreted the cryptic message? Despite the growing feeling of uncertainty within her, Emma knew that there was more to this encounter than met the eye. Fred's cryptic message, his curious smile, and the unspoken connection between them had ignited a spark within her that she couldn't ignore. And so, in spite of the incongruity of the setting, Emma resolved to take the plunge and see where this twist of fate would lead her.

Fred's eyes lit up with excitement as he spotted Emma making her way through.

With a genuine smile that reached his eyes, he quickly rose from his seat and gracefully weaved through the maze of tables to meet her. As he closed the distance, his confident strides exuded a sense of purpose. His hand was extended, offering a warm embrace of hospitality and camaraderie. Emma felt comforted and assured as she accepted his invitation to join him at the table.

With a gentle touch on her arm, Fred guided her through the maze of tightly packed chairs and tables, expertly manoeuvring through the energetic crowd. He navigated through the chaos, creating a path where there seemed to be none. The patrons, caught up in their own conversation and laughter, instinctively made way for them, sensing an air of significance that emanated from Fred's presence.

Their brief journey through the restaurant became a microcosm of their growing connection. Fred's attentiveness and careful navigation mirrored his genuine interest in Emma, ensuring that she felt comfortable and valued in his company. The din of the bustling eatery gradually faded into the background as Fred's focused attention created a sense of intimacy and exclusivity.

As they reached the table, Fred pulled out a chair for Emma with a graceful gesture, signalling that she was his honoured guest.

The surrounding patrons momentarily paused, captivated by the exchange unfolding before them. Emma, touched by Fred's chivalry and the way he effortlessly commanded the room, felt a flicker of excitement mingled with curiosity.

The atmosphere surrounding their table seemed to settle, as if the universe conspired to create a pocket of tranquillity in the midst of the restaurant's lively hustle.

For Emma, with each passing second, the fascination of the moment grew, and she leaned closer, looking deeply into Fred's eyes.

Fred's voice carried a hint of regret as he began, "Emma, I owe you an apology. I've been distant and evasive lately, and it wasn't fair to you. I want you to know that it wasn't because of anything you did. It's just... there are things happening, things I can't fully explain."

Emma's curiosity piqued, and her eyes searched Fred's face for answers. "What do you mean, Fred? What's been going on?"

Fred closed in and lowered his voice as he spoke. "I can't shake off this feeling that we're being watched, that every move we make is being scrutinized. It's been eating at me, clouding my judgement and making me act erratically. I've been afraid, Emma, afraid that I'm being monitored and that my every action has ramifications."

A flicker of concern passed over Emma's features as she reached out, placing a comforting hand on Fred's. "Fred, you don't have to face this alone. We're a team, and I'm here for you. Whatever it is, we'll figure it out together."

Fred's gaze softened, appreciating Emma's unconditional support. "Thank you, Emma. It means more to me than you know. I've been struggling with this burden, though I still believe in our work and the importance of what we're doing. But as I have minutely analysed the data, some very disturbing facts have emerged."

Emma's eyes narrowed with shock and intrigue. "What do you mean, Fred? What have you discovered?"

Fred's voice was filled with a sense of urgency. "Emma, have you ever questioned what the true objectives of the Surrogacy Program are? What do you think they're really trying to achieve?"

Emma furrowed her brow, contemplating his question. "Well, they claim it's about creating genetically superior calves, ones with stronger immunity and longer lifespans. They say it's for the betterment of agriculture and the dairy industry."

Fred interjected with a sombre expression on his face. "That's what they want us to believe. But the data I've gathered tells a totally different story, Emma. It points to a sinister agenda."

Emma gasped, curiosity and worry mingling within her. "What do you mean, Fred?

Fred inhaled deeply, choosing his words carefully. "The data I have analysed suggests that the real objective is not to create healthier calves. It's about maximizing milk production at any cost. They want cows that give ten times more milk, disregarding the toll it takes on their health and lifespan."

Emma's mind raced, trying to connect the dots. "So, are you saying that they are intentionally creating cows who may have future organ failures and shortened lifespans, all in the pursuit of higher milk production?"

Fred quickly scanned around to make sure that no one was eavesdropping before he divulged another chilling discovery. "Emma, the data I've collected revealed something more, which is totally unimaginable. The cloned embryos implanted in the surrogates will develop at an accelerated pace. Instead of the usual nine months, these embryos reach full term within a matter of weeks."

Emma exclaimed, panicking. "Weeks? That's impossible! It would put the surrogates' lives at extreme risk."

Fred affirmed, his expression grave. "Exactly, Emma. The surrogates are not biologically equipped to withstand such rapid growth and strain."

"The prognosis is grim. They won't survive the ordeal."

He paused, briefly collecting his thoughts, before continuing. "Through my data, I've discovered that the genetic modifications in these cloned cows have unintended side effects. The milk they produce contains altered proteins and hormones that could potentially disrupt the delicate balance of our own biology if consumed."

Emma's mind raced, grappling with the implications of Fred's revelation. "Are you saying that consuming this milk could have negative health effects on humans?"

Fred said it with a cautionary tone. "Yes, exactly. We're playing with forces we don't fully understand. It's crucial that the public is aware of the potential risks and side-effects of consuming GMO milk."

Fred continued, "I mustered the courage to approach Dr. Victoria, hoping to bring clarity to my findings. I needed answers and reassurances that there was a noble purpose behind all of this. And that Shanti's life, those of the future surrogates, and us humans are not endangered."

With trepidation in her heart, Emma fixed her eyes on Fred. "And what did she say? Did she acknowledge your concerns?"

A pained expression crossed Fred's face as he shook his head. "No, Emma. Dr. Victoria's reaction was far from what I expected. Instead of addressing my doubts and fears, she became defensive, dismissing my evidence as mere speculation. She accused me of undermining the integrity of the program."

Emma's face creased with disbelief. "But why would she react that way? If everything is as it seems, shouldn't she welcome scrutiny and provide explanations?"

Fred groaned, his voice heavy with disappointment. "That's what troubled me, Emma. Her defensive reaction only deepened my suspicions. It was as if she had something to hide, as if she was more concerned with protecting the program's reputation than addressing the legitimate concerns I had raised."

Fred shuddered as he revealed the shocking turn of events. "Emma, immediately after that conversation with Dr. Victoria, everything changed. Without any explanation, you were promoted to the Program Lead position, and I was stripped of my access to data. They confiscated all the evidence I had gathered, leaving me with nothing."

Emma was utterly shocked by this revelation.

"But why? Why would they promote me and deny you access to the data? It doesn't make any sense."

Fred let out a frustrated sigh. "Emma, it seems they are trying to control the flow of information to silence anyone who questions their motives. By promoting you, they might think they can keep you under their watchful eye, ensuring that you won't dig any deeper into the truth."

Emma nodded as she realized the gravity of the situation. "What do you suggest, Fred?"

Fred reached into his pocket, retrieving a small pendrive. He placed it gently in Emma's hand and muttered, "This is the only thing I could save. It contains some of the data I analysed. While it's not sufficient, it will be a good start. You need to go through it carefully, but remember, we can't afford to raise any suspicions."

Instinctively closing her fist to hide the pendrive, Emma said, "I understand, Fred. I'll examine the data discreetly and connect the dots. We need to find concrete evidence to be sure if there is any dark side to the Surrogacy program."

Fred's hands shook as he reached for the glass of ice-cold water, his nerves evident in his unsteady grip.

With a quick gulp, he attempted to calm his racing heart as he looked deep into Emma's eyes.

His heart faltered with fear and longing. It was a moment of vulnerability, a leap of faith that could either bring them closer together or push them apart.

"Emma," he began, his voice soft yet filled with sincerity. "There is one more thing that I need to tell you. It is as though my heart will explode if I keep it any longer."

Pausing briefly, he continued, "I can't deny the strong feelings that have grown within me, the way my heart races every time I see you, or the way your smile lights up my world. In the midst of this chaos, I've come to realize that I have fallen deeply, irrevocably in love with you."

Emma felt overwhelmed by a flood of emotions, finding it difficult to take it all in.

She held her breath as Fred continued. "But, Emma," Fred said, his voice tinged with pain, "as much as it hurts me to say this, I fear that our romance could be ill-fated. I can't bear the thought of anything happening to you because of our connection."

Emma's heart sank, and she reached out to grasp Fred's hand, her touch a gentle reassurance.

Tears glistened in her eyes, words failed her as her heart ached.

Fred's eyes welled up, and he brought her hand to his lips, pressing a tender kiss against her skin.

"I love you, Emma," he whispered, his voice filled with a sense of regret and warmth. "I promise you, once all this is over, I will make up for all the lost time. You have my word, Emma, we'll create memories that will be etched in our hearts forever."

A gentle smile graced Emma's lips, radiating love and understanding. She moved closer to Fred, their foreheads touching as they shared an intimate moment of connection.

"Until that day comes, Fred, let's channel our love into our work. Let's uncover the truth together. And when the time is right, we'll create a love story that's even more powerful than we ever imagined."

They were rudely interrupted by Emma's blinking phone screen. She glanced at the caller ID and saw it was Lisa, Dr. Victoria's secretary.

Reluctantly, she answered the call and listened to the rushing voice at the other end. "Dr. Victoria wants you to report to work at 8am tomorrow morning for an urgent team meeting. It seems something important has come up. Do I have your confirmation?"

"I see," Emma responded, her voice betraying a hint of distraction. "Thank you for letting me know. I'll be there without fail."

As she hung up the phone, Emma turned to Fred, her eyes filled with deep worry.

"Fred, did you receive any notification about this meeting?"

Fred quickly checked his phone and said," No, I haven't. It's strange, isn't it?"

"It surely is. It almost feels like a deliberate omission", Emma responded.

Fred bent forward, his voice barely above a whisper as he spoke. "Emma, I think it's best if you leave now, discreetly. Take the pendrive with you and review the data on your own."

"We can't risk getting caught together here. And I promise you, our next date will be everything you desire and more."

With a lingering touch and a promise in their hearts, Emma made her way out of the restaurant, clutching the pendrive tightly.

Fred watched her leave, his mind already racing with plans for their next rendezvous. His love for Emma knew no bounds. He was willing to traverse treacherous paths, brave the darkest storms, and face insurmountable odds to protect and fight for their precious love, even if it meant challenging fate itself.

Chapter 11

The Illusion of Innocence

As the morning sunlight seeped through her curtains, Emma's eyes gently opened. The warm glow that spread across her room seemed to portend a promising day ahead. She stretched her arms and felt a strange sense of elation pulsing through her.

Her mind gently replayed the memories of the previous evening spent with Fred. In Fred's presence, Emma felt a warmth envelop her.

There was a gentle tenderness in his touch, a magnetism that drew her closer, beckoning her to explore the uncharted territories of love.

Emma marvelled at the way Fred saw her, truly saw her, in all her complexity and vulnerability. It was as if he held a key to the depths of her soul, unlocking layers she didn't know existed. In his eyes, she found a reflection of her own hopes, dreams, and fears—a mirror that reflected her essence.

As she got out of bed, a song played softly in her heart, its melody uplifting her spirits and making her feel like everything was aligning perfectly in a harmonious symphony.

Suddenly, a jolt of realization struck her—the pendrive! It had momentarily slipped from her mind, but now it resurfaced with renewed urgency. She couldn't risk leaving it exposed, vulnerable to prying eyes or accidental discovery.

Emma surveyed her surroundings, seeking the perfect hiding place. Her gaze settled on an inconspicuous crevice behind a loose floorboard near her desk. Cautiously, she knelt down and lifted the loose floorboard, revealing the hidden compartment beneath. Nimbly, she slid the pendrive into the narrow space, ensuring its concealment.

As Emma carefully replaced the floorboard, she made a mental note to revisit the data later that night. Her curiosity burned within her, urging her to uncover the secrets hidden within those digital files.

As Emma stepped into the shower, the warm water cascaded over her body, soothing her tired muscles and washing away her anxiety. The steam filled the bathroom, enveloping her in a cosy embrace and creating an intimate space where her thoughts could roam freely. Her mind conjured images of Fred's smile and his eyes sparkling with intelligence and mischief. The memory of their stolen moments together lingered in her thoughts, igniting a gentle warmth deep within her heart.

As she tied the sash around her bathrobe, her thoughts turned to the challenges they faced. The lab's surveillance and the constant need for caution seemed quite overwhelming. Every interaction with Fred had to be carefully crafted. Emma knew that one slip, one momentary lapse in their act, could unravel everything they had carefully built.

Leaving the bathroom, Emma carried with her a sense of longing and a heart filled with love. Today would be another chapter in their hidden romance, a chapter filled with stolen moments, whispered confessions, and a love that defied the boundaries of their circumstances.

She gave herself a final glance in the mirror, her thoughts consumed by the image of Fred's face, his eyes reflecting the same emotions that danced within her, and stepped out of her home. The day felt precious, as it held the promise of a future where their love could finally be free.

As Emma walked briskly on the street, her instincts urged her to glance over her shoulder, and she obliged, casting a quick furtive look to see if someone was tailing her. There was no one, but as Emma continued to walk, their footsteps seemed to echo in the recesses of her mind. She tried to rationalize it, attributing the sensation to the stress of recent events.

But deep down, a primal instinct cautioned that there was more to it.

The weight of the unknown pressed upon her, intensifying like a storm brewing on the horizon, leaving her on edge and perpetually vigilant. She knew she couldn't afford to ignore her instincts; they had never let her down.

As Emma reached the lab, a stoic silence surrounded the empty workstations. She made her way towards the conference room, a hunch guiding her steps.

The door swung open, revealing a solemn scene. The room was filled with her colleagues, their expressions marked with concern and tension. At the front of the room stood Dr. Victoria, her typically composed disposition now masked by a grave seriousness.

Emma took a seat among her fellow team members, her eyes searching for Fred's familiar face. But he was nowhere to be seen, adding to her growing sense of distress.

Dr. Victoria stood before the grim-faced team, her voice carrying a sombre note as she delivered the shocking news.

"I regret to inform you all that our dear colleague and friend, Fred Astridge, met with an untimely and tragic accident in the early hours of this morning. It is with heavy hearts that we mourn his sudden passing."

"Our thoughts and condolences go out to his family during this unimaginably difficult time."

The room erupted in a cacophony of gasps and murmurs, the collective shock reverberating through the walls. Emma's vision blurred as tears welled up in her eyes, threatening to spill over. The world around her seemed to spin.

Dr. Victoria continued, "In light of the circumstances, GenED has decided to respect the wishes of Fred's family for privacy and has agreed not to attend the memorial service. It is important that we honour their request and give them the space they need to grieve."

Dr. Victoria's voice seemed to drift from a far-off place, hollow and distant, as she continued to speak, detailing the tragic circumstances that claimed Fred's life. Emma struggled to comprehend the details, her mind engulfed in numbing disbelief, as if she were trapped in a surreal nightmare.

"Fred was a valued member of our team, and his contributions will never be forgotten. We owe it to him to carry on his work and ensure that his dedication and passion for science live on. As we move forward, I will be entrusting Emma with the responsibility of overseeing the development of the first cloned calf, a project that Fred was deeply invested in."

"Emma, you have shown exceptional dedication and capability in your role. We believe in your ability to carry on Fred's important work."

"The first cloned calf will be born in just a few weeks instead of nine long months. We need someone who understands the project intimately to ensure its success."

As Dr. Victoria's words echoed in Emma's mind, a chilling revelation crept over her: Fred's accident was definitely not an accident; it was a carefully orchestrated and deliberate act of violence aimed at silencing him and concealing the truth.

The urgency with which Fred had shared his findings, the fear in his eyes, and Dr. Victoria's sudden dismissal of his concerns all painted a sinister picture. Someone within the lab, someone with immense power and influence, had executed Fred's demise to protect their secrets.

Emma stood before Dr. Victoria, her eyes filled with deep grief and shock that she struggled to conceal. She fought to hide her emotions, knowing that showing them would not serve her purpose. She spoke slowly, trying to mask her searing pain. "Thank you, Dr. Victoria, for entrusting me with this responsibility. I am deeply saddened by the loss of Fred. But I assure you, I will do everything in my power to honour his memory and continue the work he believed in so passionately."

Dr. Victoria, ever observant, studied Emma's face for any signs of vulnerability and said with a cold stare. "Emma, I understand that this is a difficult time for all of us, but we must stay focused on the task at hand."

Despite her heart weighing heavy with anger and grief, Emma nodded. She had to tread carefully, for she knew that Dr. Victoria's true intentions remained veiled in secrecy and deception. She couldn't afford to reveal her true emotions, not when the stakes were so high. She spoke up in a firm tone: "I will do my best to continue Fred's work, Dr. Victoria. It's what he would have wanted."

As Dr. Victoria's discerning gaze bore into her, Emma felt as though her soul was being scrutinized. However, she summoned all her strength and managed to maintain her composure, concealing the turmoil that raged within her.

As she stepped out of the conference room, Emma's mind was overwhelmed with a torrent of emotions. With a sense of urgency, she dashed towards Shanti's Enclosure where the surrogate was strapped to monitoring devices for constant observation after the implant.

With grief weighing heavily on her heart, Emma approached Shanti's side, her trembling hand reaching out to stroke the cow's soft hide.

Each touch carried sorrow, longing, and an unspoken connection that transcended words.

As her fingers glided along Shanti's flank, Emma could feel the warmth of the animal's presence, a silent reassurance in the midst of her pain.

In that intimate exchange, Emma poured her grief into Shanti, as if the cow could bear the weight of her sorrow. With each stroke, she released a fragment of the anguish that consumed her, finding a fleeting respite in the cow's silent companionship. Shanti, though bound by monitoring devices, exuded a soothing energy, as if offering a comforting embrace to Emma's grieving soul.

With teary eyes, Emma looked into Shanti's gentle eyes, her voice choked with remorse. "I'm so sorry, Shanti, I didn't know... I didn't realize the dangers you were facing. I should have protected you."

Her hand continued to stroke Shanti's hide, each touch imbued with apology and tenderness. The weight of her regret felt heavy upon her as she gazed at the cow, longing to erase the pain she now knew had been inflicted upon her.

"I never wanted any harm to come to you," Emma continued, her voice laced with sadness. "I thought I was doing what was best, but now I see the truth. The dangers, the risks—they were all hidden from me. And I'm so sorry that you've had to bear the consequences."

Tears welled up in Emma's eyes, spilling over onto her cheeks as she sought forgiveness in Shanti's gaze.

"I promise, Shanti," Emma whispered, "I will make things right. I won't let anyone else suffer because of the secrets they hide."

With one final touch, Emma gently withdrew her hand, a lingering connection still felt between them. She stepped back, carrying the weight of her apology and her promise to Shanti. It was a silent understanding, an unspoken bond that would guide her in the days to come.

As Emma stepped out of Shanti's enclosure, her grief transformed into a burning fire, fuelling her quest for justice. She knew she couldn't trust anyone within the confines of the lab, where secrets and shadows concealed the truth. The more she thought about it, the more convinced she became that there were powerful forces at play, willing to go to great lengths to ensure their secrets remained buried.

With her heart heavy and her mind focused, Emma promised to carry on with Fred's mission.

She would honour his memory by uncovering the truth and exposing the dark underbelly of the lab.

She knew it would be a dangerous path, but she was no longer afraid.

As Emma made her way back to her desk, her senses heightened. Every shadow, every creaking floorboard, seemed to echo a warning. She became acutely aware that she was being watched and that her every move was being monitored. But she refused to be intimidated. If they thought they could silence her like they had silenced Fred, they were gravely mistaken.

She knew that exposing the truth came at a great personal risk, but she couldn't turn her back on the injustice that had claimed Fred's life. With every step she took, she felt Fred's presence guiding her and urging her forward.

Emma knew that the road ahead would be fraught with perils and obstacles, but she was prepared to face them all for the love she had lost and the justice she sought.

The forces that have conspired against Fred and Shanti will soon realize that they have awakened a formidable adversary in Emma.

Chapter 12

The Countdown

Emma's heartbeat hastened as she hurriedly made her way back to her apartment, her mind filled with a sense of urgency. Time was of the essence, as every passing minute brought her closer to uncovering the truth hidden within the depths of Fred's data. Emma cautiously slid open the hidden compartment to retrieve the safely stashed pendrive.

As she inserted the pendrive into her laptop, she felt a sense of dread coursing through her veins. The soft hum of the device coming to life echoed in the silent room, its glow illuminating her face. Emma's eyes focused intently on the screen, her fingers dancing across the keyboard as she delved deep into the labyrinth of Fred's data.

Hour after hour, she painstakingly sifted through the digital archives, unearthing fragments of information and piecing together the puzzle that had consumed her thoughts.

The night slipped away unnoticed as Emma's grit propelled her forward.

She pored over lines of code, scanned through research files, and dissected cryptic notes, driven by a thirst for answers.

The hours melted into the early light of dawn as Emma delved deeper into the heart of Fred's research. The truth unfolded like a chilling tale, with each piece of information more disturbing than the last.

With a sinking feeling in the pit of her stomach, Emma discovered that the cloned calf's gestation period had been dramatically accelerated. Instead of the usual nine months, it was scheduled to be born within a mere ninety days. The implications were clear—such a rapid development would put an enormous strain on the surrogate mother, rendering her unable to survive the process. Less than 5% of the surrogates would survive the birthing process.

And the implications didn't end there.

Emma discovered the dark intentions behind the project—to produce a staggering 1,000 cloned animals by the end of the year. The sheer scale of the operation was astounding. To achieve this, 2,000 animals would need to be produced, as only half of them would survive the cloning process.

The rest would suffer from severe deformities and organ failures, condemned to a life of suffering.

Overcome by sheer desperation, Emma whispered into the stark silence. "Who's behind all this? What's the end game?"

As she dug deeper, the data revealed a chilling truth: these animals were being genetically engineered to become Super Cows. Their immunity levels would be vastly superior, and their milk production activity would be amplified tenfold. The pursuit of profit and power has blinded those involved to the grave implications and the toll it would take on innocent lives.

As the weight of the information settled upon her, Emma was overcome with anger, disbelief, and a deep sense of responsibility. She understood the urgency of the situation. Lives were at stake—both for the animals subjected to this cruel experiment and for the unknowing consumers who would ingest the genetically modified products.

This was a battle against the exploitation of science and the manipulation of nature for selfish gains. Emma knew that she held a small piece of the puzzle. And with this knowledge came the burden of choice—to go all the way to put together the missing pieces of the puzzle—to expose the truth, to protect the innocent, and to confront those responsible.

Emma's mind raced with the urgency of her mission.

With the clock ticking down to the birth of the first cloned calf, she knew she had a limited window of opportunity to gather evidence, build a case, and expose the perpetrators responsible for this heinous project.

She understood the importance of discretion, knowing that any slip-up or suspicion raised could sabotage her mission. Emma scrupulously planned her actions, ensuring she left no trace of her investigation. She would document every piece of evidence, from files and data to correspondence and recordings, storing them in secure locations known only to her.

Emma realised that the cloned calf being born after only 90 days was irrefutable proof of the twisted scheme orchestrated by Dr. Victoria and her accomplices.

Emma made a resolute decision to wait patiently until the calf's arrival. This would be the undeniable evidence she needed to expose the dark secrets hidden within GenED. Every passing day would feel like an eternity, but Emma knew that she must bide her time, gather more information, and ensure the truth would be revealed at the right moment.

With her mind set and her heart aflame with conviction, Emma prepared herself for the battle ahead.

The journey would be arduous, demanding unimaginable sacrifices, but she was determined to see it through.

For the sake of the innocent, for the protection of ethics and integrity in science, and for Fred and Shanti, Emma would work tirelessly to expose the ones responsible and bring them to justice.

Emma expertly masked her true intentions at the lab, seamlessly blending into the daily routine while discreetly gathering evidence. With a smile on her face and a keen eye, she observed the activities around her and noted every suspicious interaction and anomaly. She engaged in casual conversations, carefully extracting information that would aid her cause. She catalogued files, subtly snapped photos when no one was watching, and copied confidential documents under the guise of routine tasks.

With each passing day, Emma skilfully deepened her façade of loyalty and dedication to her work.

She strategically positioned herself as Dr. Victoria's most trusted assistant, always delivering impeccable results and offering unwavering support.

Her ability to gain Dr. Victoria's trust became her greatest asset, allowing her to access restricted areas and confidential data without raising suspicion.

With just a day left before the arrival of the cloned calf, Emma's anxiety intensified. She had managed to gather substantial evidence, but there was one crucial file that remained elusive: the one that links the potential use of cloned animals to bio-warfare. This file held the key to justice and the hope of saving countless lives from the horrors of bio-warfare.

As per Fred's data, she should be able to locate this file in Restricted Area A.

The entrance to this area was adjacent to Dr. Victoria's office, and the risks of being caught were exponentially higher. She knew that attempting to breach the highly secure area could be suicidal, but she had reached a critical juncture in her mission.

Back at her apartment, Emma sat glued to the blueprint of the lab, hoping to find a way to infiltrate Restricted Area A. The restricted area was marked with bold red lines, indicating the high-security measures in place.

She studied the security protocols minutely, identifying potential weak points and vulnerabilities. She knew that timing and stealth would be her allies in this mission. She needed to find a way to bypass the security systems undetected.

After hours of careful planning, Emma devised a plan.

She would take advantage of a scheduled maintenance window when the security systems would be temporarily disabled.

It was a narrow window of opportunity, but it was her best chance to enter the restricted area unnoticed.

As the designated time arrived, Emma made her way towards the restricted area. She moved rapidly, her steps measured and purposeful.

She had memorized the patrol patterns of the security guards and synchronized her movements with their routine.

Using her knowledge of the lab's layout, Emma navigated through corridors and passages, relying on her intuition to lead her closer to her objective. She moved silently, aware of every creaking floorboard and distant footstep.

Finally, she reached the entrance to the restricted area. As she approached the advanced biometric security system, she flashed the stolen security credentials and swiftly bypassed the system, gaining access.

Inside the restricted area, Emma's senses heightened. She knew that time was ticking and she had to act expeditiously. She moved with agility, her eyes scanning for the specific cabinet that held the valuable information she sought. Carefully and quietly, she opened the cabinet.

After a few excruciating seconds, she spotted the file. Retrieving it in one fell swoop, she concealed it under her sweater. As Emma prepared to leave, she was startled by the sound of approaching footsteps. Her heart skipped a beat as Dr. Victoria appeared, a stern expression etched on her face.

Emma's pulse quickened, and she braced herself for a potential confrontation.

Dr. Victoria's gaze bore into Emma, trying to assess her true motives. There was a split-second of tense silence as the two women came face-to-face, each assessing the other's intentions. Emma's mind galloped, searching for the right words to say and the right guise to display.

Finally, Dr. Victoria broke the silence, her voice laced with a controlled sternness. "Emma," she said firmly, "What brings you to this part of the facility? This area is strictly off-limits to personnel without proper authorization."

Emma's heart pounded in her chest as she weighed her response. She was acutely aware that a single fumble would derail everything she had worked for. With a calm yet slightly nervous tone, she replied, "I apologize, Dr. Victoria. I was just trying to find some additional information related to the project we've been working on. I thought I might find it here."

Dr. Victoria's eyes narrowed, her gaze piercing through Emma's façade. She studied her carefully, seemingly assessing the truthfulness of her words. After a moment of tense scrutiny, Dr. Victoria sighed, her expression softening ever so slightly, her voice still tinged with a hint of caution. "But the nature of our work demands strict confidentiality. It is imperative that you respect the boundaries and protocols we have in place."

Emma nodded, her heart still racing. She knew she had narrowly avoided suspicion, but she couldn't let her guard down.

"I apologize for my intrusion, Dr. Victoria," Emma replied, her voice laced with sincerity. "You're right, and I'll make sure to adhere to the protocols from now on."

Dr. Victoria's gaze lingered on Emma for a moment longer before she finally spoke. "See that you do, Emma," she said, her tone carrying a note of warning. "The work we do here is of paramount importance, and any breach of trust will not be taken lightly. You need to leave immediately."

With that final admonition, Dr. Victoria escorted Emma out of the area.

The facility's corridors felt like a labyrinth of secrets, and Emma moved with cautious precision.

Dr. Victoria's warning reverberated in her mind like a haunting melody.

Emma clearly understood that she was now walking a tightrope. Every step she took and every move she made had to be calculated and deliberate. She knew that the walls had eyes, and any misstep would not only compromise her mission but also her safety. Dr. Victoria was a formidable force, and underestimating her could be fatal.

As Emma stepped out into the cool night air, a sense of relief washed over her.

In the privacy of the darkened streets, Emma let the tears flow freely, a blend of exhaustion, fear, and the overwhelming weight of her mission.

Under the blanket of a star-studded sky, Emma found herself gazing upward, seeking comfort in the vastness of the universe. The twinkling stars above reminded her of Fred, a guiding light who had left this world too soon. But in her heart, she knew that his presence lingered, watching over her like a guardian angel.

Emma had come so far, overcome countless obstacles, and braved unimaginable dangers. And now, with the cloned calf just a day away, the final proof awaited. She was ready to bear witness to the birth that would expose the truth and set into motion a chain of events that could reshape the future.

c-314A is here

In the early hours of the morning, when darkness still blanketed the world, Emma's phone blared. Groggy but alert, she picked up the call. The voice on the other end urgently requested her presence at the birthing chamber. A gush of expectancy coursed through her being. She knew that today was the day—the day she would take a monumental risk to uncover the truth. Her hand reached under her pillow, and she retrieved the spy pen camera.

Knowing that no electronic devices would be permitted in the secured area, Emma ingeniously planned her strategy. She dressed with extreme care, ensuring the spy pen camera was concealed within her clothing. As she approached the security checkpoint, Emma felt her heart quicken.

The security personnel scrutinized her belongings with keen eyes, their gaze lingering on her as they searched for any signs of forbidden technology.

Emma's palms grew clammy; she held her breath, praying that her carefully concealed spy pen camera would go unnoticed.

Time seemed to stand still as the security personnel finished their inspection, their expressions inscrutable. Emma's relief was almost tangible when they motioned for her to proceed.

The tension that had coiled within Emma's body slowly began to release, giving way to a deep sense of relief. She had cleared the first hurdle. With each step she took towards the birthing chamber, her confidence grew. The spy pen camera, her silent ally, nestled securely against her.

The birthing chamber stood as a square, transparent enclosure, its glass walls providing a glimpse into the extraordinary events that were about to unfold.

The enclosure was designed to allow observers a clear view of the process, a spectacle that would forever change the course of NectarMeadow.

Emma stepped inside the chamber to give a few final instructions to the technicians. The technicians double-checked their instruments, ensuring that every detail was in perfect order. Their eyes darted from monitors to screens, verifying the stability of vital signs and confirming the readiness of the equipment.

The chamber was awash in soft, diffused light that imbued the space with a gentle glow. The air held a tangible anticipation, as if aware of the significance of the impending birth.

Shanti, secured by soft yet unyielding straps, stood at the heart of the birthing chamber. The soft glow of light embraced her sleek coat, accentuating her grace. Unaware of the sinister web that ensnared her, Shanti stood, exuding an aura of innocence and vulnerability.

As Emma neared Shanti, her heart felt heavy with a deep sense of sorrow. She extended a hand, allowing her fingers to graze Shanti's side, feeling the warmth of her presence. Emma murmured words of comfort and farewell, her voice laced with love and regret. "Shanti," her voice barely audible in the hushed ambiance of the chamber, "farewell, I am sorry; I could not protect you." As if sensing the weight of Emma's words, Shanti turned her large, gentle eyes towards her. In that gaze lay the recognition of the shared fate they had been bound to.

Emma gently withdrew her hand and stepped back, taking one last lingering look at Shanti. Shanti's memory would forever be etched in her heart.

Through the transparent glass walls of the birthing chamber, Emma caught sight of Dr. Victoria slowly making her way towards the centre.

Wiping her tears in a swift decision to allay any suspicions, Emma stepped out and greeted her with a warm smile.

"Good morning, Dr. Victoria," Emma said, her voice calm and composed. "It's an exciting day, isn't it?"

Dr. Victoria nodded, a hint of a smile crossing her face. "I couldn't agree more, Emma. The culmination of our hard work is finally here."

Emma helped Dr. Victoria settle into her seat, strategically positioning herself at the opposite end to have a clear view of her through the glass. With each passing minute, Emma's grip tightened around the spy pen camera, and she flicked it on.

As the team members began to fill the observer seats around them, Emma maintained a friendly and engaging persona, occasionally stealing glances at Dr. Victoria and observing her every move and gesture.

Malcolm walked into the birthing chamber a few seconds later, his nerves palpable as he took the seat next to Dr. Victoria. With agitation and anxiety written on his face, he nervously adjusted himself, trying to find a comfortable position.

As Malcolm settled into his seat, Dr. Victoria glanced at him briefly, her expression cool and composed. Emma's perceptive eyes caught a fleeting undercurrent of tension between them. Emma wondered what could be causing Malcolm's nervousness. Was he aware of the true nature of the experiments being conducted at NectarMeadow? What was the extent of his involvement? Did he suspect Dr. Victoria's ulterior motives? Or was he simply overwhelmed by the weight of the situation unfolding before him?

However, Emma knew better than to rely solely on assumptions. She had learned from experience that trust must be earned, especially in a world shrouded in secrecy and deception. She decided to observe Malcolm closely, looking for any signs of resistance or a crack in his allegiance to Dr. Victoria.

As the final seconds approached, the observers pitched forward, eager to witness history in the making.

And the moment finally arrived—the calf emerged into the world. The room erupted with a collective gasp as the wet and trembling newborn took its first breath. Emma, positioned strategically across from Dr. Victoria, carefully aimed the pen camera, capturing the momentous event frame by frame.

The sight was breath-taking.

The calf, coated in a glistening film, struggled to find its footing on tottering legs. Its eyes blinked open, revealing a world filled with curious onlookers.

Despite the torture that ravaged her body, Shanti's maternal instincts surged forth.

Though she lay on the floor, Shanti mustered the strength to extend her neck and nuzzle her calf. Her large, gentle tongue delicately caressed the calf's sleek coat, as if assuring it of her love and protection. Every lick and every touch spoke volumes about the unbreakable bond between mother and child.

And in just a few minutes, the calf, a product of genetic manipulation and scientific prowess, stood tall, its eyes scanning the room, seemingly aware of the significance of the moment.

A hushed murmur swept through the room as the team marvelled at the sight before them. The calf's coat glistened with an almost ethereal sheen; its features were a testament to the precision and ingenuity of the cloning process.

It was a surreal blend of the familiar and the unknown, a living testament to the boundaries that science dared to push.

With each passing second, it became evident that Shanti's strength was waning.

The life that had coursed through her veins now flickered faintly.

Recognizing the gravity of the situation, the GenED team acted promptly to remove Shanti from the birthing chamber.

As Emma sensed the distress emanating from the calf due to separation from Shanti, she bolted from her seat, approaching the team of technicians. "Team, we need to initiate the weaning protocol immediately; the calf is showing signs of separation anxiety."

With practiced moves, the technicians created a soothing environment in the birthing chamber, carefully adjusting the temperature and humidity to mimic the warmth and comfort the calf had experienced within the safety of its mother's womb. Soft, comforting sounds filled the air, replicating the rhythmic beats and murmurs that had once serenaded the calf in Shanti's womb.

c-314A has finally arrived.

Chapter 14

Appealing to the Voice

Emma felt consumed by a maelstrom of thoughts and emotions as she hastily made her way back home, bypassing the GenED celebration party. The images of the birthing chamber, the awe-inspiring birth of the calf, and the listless body of Shanti weighed heavily on her mind.

As she entered her quiet and dimly lit apartment, she knew that another sleepless night awaited her, and she reached out for her cup of coffee. As she surveyed her desk, strewn with stacks of papers and notes, she slipped back into the chair, clutching the warm mug between her hands and letting the steam caress her face.

With a resolute focus, she began to piece together the fragments of evidence, connecting the dots to unveil the sinister conspiracy.

Every document, photograph, and recorded conversation served as a stark reminder of the horrors she had witnessed and the urgent need to bring them to light.

In the solitude of her thoughts, Emma carefully weighed her options, aware that the course she chose would have far-reaching repercussions. She knew that she held a double-edged sword— one side a tool for justice, the other a potential weapon against her own safety.

Her first instinct was to find an ally in Malcolm and the GenED team members and expose Dr. Victoria.

But having closely observed Malcolm at the birthing chamber, Emma understood that Malcolm was under the influence of Dr. Victoria and may or may not be fully aware of the extent of the dark agenda. Confronting him directly might risk pushing him further into the depths of denial. The GenED team, including Malcolm, had likely been carefully chosen by Dr. Victoria for their loyalty and compliance. Approaching them might lead to them closing ranks and protecting each other, making it harder to dismantle the corrupt system at NectarMeadow. Emma needed to build a broader case against the entire operation.

Next, Emma considered approaching the authorities, seeking their intervention in this web of deceit.

Law enforcement agencies had the resources and jurisdiction to launch investigations and hold those responsible accountable.

However, she couldn't ignore the possibility of corruption or collusion that might taint the pursuit of justice.

After carefully weighing her options, Emma came to a firm decision. She understood that the best way to ensure her findings reached the widest audience and had the greatest impact was by going public through the power of the media.

By focusing on the power of public awareness and leveraging the media's reach, Emma aimed to ignite a collective call for justice and reform. The fact that this path would be challenging and laden with risks was not lost on Emma. She was well aware of the potential backlash, threats, and attempts to discredit her work that awaited her on this path.

But Emma also believed in the power of the collective voice. She hoped that by exposing the unethical practices and the hidden truth, she could rally public support and bring about change. The media had the reach and influence to disseminate her story far and wide, sparking outrage.

She needed to alert the public to the potential danger and threat. Paint a vivid picture of the suffering endured by innocent animals and the dangers posed to the health of consumers.

But most of all, reveal the extent of deception perpetrated by GenED.

With fiery tenacity, Emma began strategizing her media approach.

She carefully selected reputable journalists and publications known for their commitment to investigative journalism and truth-seeking. For the numerous names that appeared on her screen, Emma researched their previous articles, their approach towards uncovering corruption and injustice, and their allegiances and networks.

After hours of painstaking research, one name stood out—Sarah Anderson, an investigative reporter from GlobalPost.

She knew that establishing contact with Sarah would be no easy feat. The risks were high, and the surveillance on her every move made it nearly impossible to communicate without detection. The mere thought of it was intimidating and dismaying.

She paced restlessly, her mind playing out all the potential scenarios that could go wrong.

What if her message fell into the wrong hands?

What if her identity was revealed even before the truth?

What if she is endangering Sarah's life?

The fallout could be catastrophic, not just for her but for the truth she so desperately sought to expose.

As Emma stood in her apartment, her nerves on edge and her mind filled with uncertainty, she felt a strong need to find some respite and regain her composure. The weight of her mission and the constant surveillance had taken their toll, leaving her mentally and emotionally drained.

She decided that a warm shower might be just the thing to bring some semblance of calmness to her restless spirit.

The gentle drizzle of the water wrapped her in a warm cuddle. In this serene space, Emma strongly felt a familiar presence surrounding her—Fred. She felt transported to that moment in the bustling restaurant, where, ever so gently, Fred had whispered to her, "I love you, Emma. You have my word; we'll create memories that will be etched in our hearts forever." Emma closed her eyes, letting the rhythmic sound of the water wash away her worries.

As she stepped out of the shower, an idea began to take shape.

Walking back to her desk, Emma opened her laptop and began researching online communication channels that offered encryption and anonymity.

After thorough consideration, she decided to utilize a secure platform known for protecting user privacy and create an anonymous account.

The sun began to rise, ushering in a new day. She had to report to the lab in the next half hour.

As she stepped out, the air felt crisp, and a cool breeze brushed against her face. The deserted streets were slowly coming alive with the hum of traffic and the bustle of pedestrians.

Emma navigated through the busy streets, her pace brisk and purposeful, and stepped into a small electronics store tucked away in a quiet corner. Her pulse quickened as she approached the counter, trying to appear inconspicuous. The store clerk, a middle-aged man with a bored expression, glanced up as Emma approached. "Can I help you?" he asked in a monotone voice.

Emma nodded, trying to keep her nerves in check. "I need a burner phone," she mumbled, making sure no one else could overhear.

The clerk eyed her suspiciously, assessing her intentions. After a momentary pause, he reached under the counter and retrieved a small box. He placed it on the counter and pushed it towards Emma. With uncertain hands, Emma opened the box. Inside, she found a simple, nondescript phone—the type that wouldn't raise any eyebrows.

It had minimal features, but that was all she needed.

Emma walked briskly, her senses on high alert, vigilant for surveillance, blending in seamlessly with the crowd.

She found a small café nestled among the busy shops and decided it would be the perfect place to make the call.

Seating herself at a corner table, Emma glanced around, ensuring no one was paying particular attention to her. She reached into her pocket and pulled out a slip of paper with Sarah's contact information, carefully handwritten to avoid leaving digital traces.

With tentative fingers, she dialled the number, her heart racing with each ring.

Emma: (nervously) Hello, Sarah? I have some crucial information about GenED labs set up clandestinely at NectarMeadow that needs to be exposed.

Sarah: (curiously) Who is this? How did you get my number?

Emma: It doesn't matter right now. What's important is that we talk. Lives are at stake, Sarah.

Sarah: (concerned) Okay. I'm listening. What's going on?

Emma: (whispering) I'm an insider, and I have evidence of dangerous and life-threatening practices at GenED. Cloning, genetic manipulation, bio-warfare—the works. They're endangering lives, Sarah. We need to expose them.

Sarah: (hushed) Are you sure about this? These are serious allegations. Why are you coming to me?

Emma: (determined) I've seen your work, Sarah. I know you have the courage and integrity to bring this to light. We can't trust anyone else. We need someone who can dig deep and expose the truth.

Sarah: Can you guarantee the authenticity of the evidence?

Emma: I'll provide you with everything I have— documents, recordings, everything. But we can't meet in person. It will endanger both of our lives.

Sarah: Alright. I would like to take a look at all the evidence. How can we communicate securely?

Emma: You will receive an anonymous email tonight at 8pm sharp.

Sarah: Right. But please don't try contacting me in the future. If the evidence you have truly carries weight, I will get back to you.

With that, Sarah ended the call abruptly, leaving Emma with a cloud of uncertainty.

She knew that she had taken a big gamble by reaching out to the media, and it was now an agonising waiting game.

Just then Emma's work phone buzzed; it was Dr. Victoria's secretary.

Emma hastily yanked the battery out of the burner phone before answering.

"Emma, Dr. Victoria would like to see you in the conference room in the next hour". The secretary's voice sounded authoritative.

Suppressing her anxiety, Emma replied, "Of course, I am on my way."

The burner phone felt like a ticking time bomb in her pocket. She knew she couldn't afford to keep it any longer, not with the increasing surveillance and suspicion surrounding her.

Emma hurriedly walked down the bustling street. Spotting a nearby park, Emma quickened her pace, and her fingers gripped the phone tightly. As she reached a secluded bench surrounded by trees, she retrieved a small screwdriver and began dismantling the phone, carefully removing the battery and SIM card. Every piece was vital, and she made sure to destroy them beyond recognition.

With each component safely separated, Emma scattered them in different directions, ensuring it would be impossible to retrieve, reconstruct, or trace them back to her.

But even as she took this necessary precaution, Emma couldn't cast off the macabre feeling of being watched.

Emma composed herself and, with hurried steps, resumed her journey back to the lab, on the qui vive for any signs of surveillance.

Chapter 15

The Crescent Moon

As Emma pushed open the heavy conference room door, her eyes unwittingly locked with the cold gaze of Dr. Victoria. The room fell into momentary silence as all eyes turned towards Emma. She could feel the weight of scrutiny, as if her every move was being dissected by her colleagues.

"Emma, I noticed you were not present at the celebration yesterday," Dr. Victoria said, her tone laced with a subtle blend of mistrust and intrigue. "Is there a particular reason for your absence?"

Emma gathered her thoughts, choosing her words carefully, as she met Dr. Victoria's gaze head-on. "I apologize, Dr. Victoria. I wasn't feeling too well. I think the exhaustion from months of hard work and sleepless nights finally caught up with me."

Dr. Victoria's inscrutable gaze lingered, as if trying to decipher the hidden meaning behind Emma's words. But then, totally unexpectedly, a subtle change in her countenance took place.

A twisted smile tugged at the corners of her lips, and her eyes softened with a hint of admiration.

"Emma," Dr. Victoria said, her voice now filled with a sense of genuine pride, "I must commend you on your dedication and commitment. Your work has been exemplary, and your contributions have not gone unnoticed."

As Dr. Victoria's words echoed through the room, a wave of applause erupted from the team members.

As the applause subsided, Dr. Victoria approached Emma and, leaning in closer, whispered, "We are on the cusp of something extraordinary, and your role in this cannot be underestimated. I am looking forward to working more closely with you."

Emma's mind raced like a runaway train, trying to decipher the meaning behind the cryptic words. It was an unexpected turn, for Dr. Victoria's manner seemed too calculated and precise to be mere coincidence. Emma's instincts screamed, warning her of the lurking danger.

She nodded, acknowledging Dr. Victoria's words without revealing her own inner turmoil. "I appreciate your acknowledgment," Emma replied, her voice calm and measured. "I am fully committed to the success of our endeavours."

Out of the blue, Dr. Victoria's focus was interrupted by a notification sound on her phone.

As she quickly glanced at the screen, her stance changed, transitioning to a solemn and serious expression.

Whatever she had read seemed to have caught her off guard, injecting a sense of urgency into her manner. The lines on her face deepened, betraying the weight of the news she had just received.

There was a brief hesitation in Dr. Victoria's movements, as if she were torn between addressing the matter at hand and maintaining her composed façade. She adjusted her coat, regained her authoritative presence, and began to move purposefully in the direction opposite to where Emma stood.

All eyes turned towards Dr. Victoria as she began to address the team. "I am pleased to announce that c-314A is thriving. Our efforts, coupled with the exceptional contributions of Emma and her team, have ensured its successful start in life." A murmur of satisfaction rippled through the room.

"Unfortunately, I must also share some totally unexpected news I just received. The surrogate has passed away".

A collective gasp of disbelief echoed through the room, as if the air itself had been sucked out.

The news overshadowed the previous mood of celebration.

Dr. Victoria paused, allowing the weight of the news to settle in.

Her gaze swept across the room, acknowledging the emotions reflected on each team member's face.

"I know this is a difficult and totally unanticipated loss for all of us. While we mourn the surrogate's passing, we must also remember the purpose that drives us forward. Our mission to advance scientific knowledge and benefit society remains unchanged. Let us channel our grief into a renewed commitment to continue our work."

A brief silence enveloped the room, punctuated by a collective sense of loss.

As Dr. Victoria concluded her address, the room slowly returned to a state of subdued activity. The team members exchanged glances; their eyes reflected sadness and a shared commitment to carry on the Program's objectives.

Emma hurriedly made her way to the nearby ladies' room, feeling a rush of emotions welling up inside her. Once inside the privacy of the empty restroom, she closed the door behind her and leaned against it, tears streaming down her face.

The sobs escaped her lips, echoing in the small space. Every ounce of pent-up emotion poured out as she mourned the loss of Shanti and felt haunted by the realization of the sacrifice the mother had made for the sake of the calf's existence.

In that vulnerable moment, she allowed herself to mourn not only the loss of Shanti but also the toll that the entire journey had taken on her. The physical and emotional exhaustion, the constant danger, and the secrecy all seemed to converge in this moment of raw vulnerability. Minutes felt like eternity as Emma's tears continued to flow, her emotions pouring out unchecked.

Eventually, the sobs began to subside, leaving behind a profound sense of emptiness. Emma wiped her tear-streaked face with tremulous hands and straightened her posture. Her eyes, red and swollen, encircled by the remnants of sorrow, still held the glint of tenacity.

Emma knew that she had to stay on course to honour Shanti's memory and for the sake of c-314A she had brought into this world.

With newfound strength, she splashed cold water on her face, as if washing away the physical and emotional traces of her tears.

As Emma looked at herself in the mirror once more, she saw the image of resilience staring back at her.

Walking towards the birthing chamber, Emma's steps grew more purposeful with each stride. As she reached the entrance to the chamber, she paused, peering through the transparent glass wall. Inside, c-314A stood gracefully, its inquisitive eyes flitting around the chamber as if searching for someone familiar.

As Emma approached c-314A, she sensed an uncanny familiarity. It was as if the calf recognized her, drawing her closer with a beckoning gaze. With extreme tenderness and a sense of awe, Emma extended her hand, her fingertips grazing its soft fur. As her hand glided along the calf's back, Emma couldn't help but marvel at its perfectly formed contours. Its large and gentle eyes, bright and full of curiosity, held a spark of life that mirrored the spirit of Shanti. There was a certain allure about c-314A—a captivating luminosity that seemed to transcend the ordinary. It was as though the calf embodied the very essence of Luna, the enchanting Roman goddess of the moon.

The ancient Romans believed that Luna ruled not only the celestial realms but also held sway over the mortal world. She controlled the tides, influencing the ebb and flow of the oceans, and possessed the power to transform night into day. Her most potent power was how she could sway the emotions and minds of mortals.

In her mind's eye, Emma envisioned Luna traversing the night sky in her celestial chariot with the crescent moon adorning her head.

As Emma whispered the name "c-Luna", a fusion of the calf's cloned origin and the divine spirit that seemed to emanate from within, she felt a sense of deep reverence in her heart. She knew that this name would serve as a guiding light and a beacon of hope in her journey ahead.

Back at her apartment, Emma hastily moved to her desk, where her laptop patiently awaited her. Sitting down, she logged into her anonymous email account and meticulously attached the compiled evidence to the email.

Each document and photograph were pieces of the puzzle that would expose the truth. As she reviewed the contents one final time, a burst of adrenaline in her veins egged her on.

She pressed the "send" button, the click echoing in the silence of the room as she watched her message disappear into the vast digital abyss, carrying with it the weight of the truth.

In the days that followed, Emma maintained her vigilance, careful not to arouse suspicion among her colleagues.

As she went about her daily routine, she anxiously checked her anonymous email account, yearning for a response from Sarah.

The wait felt interminable. Doubts crept into her mind. She dreaded that perhaps Sarah would never respond and that her plea for help had gone unanswered.

Chapter 16

How Far Will You Go?

Sarah Anderson sat in her cluttered office at GlobalPost, her hands clasped tightly together, immersed in deep contemplation. She was feeling overwhelmed by the enormity of the decision that faced her. As she sat surrounded by stacks of documents and the computer screen with multiple open tabs, she felt conflicted and unsure of how to progress.

She remembered the devastating aftermath of the previous whistle-blower's account and how it had cost them dearly. The legal battles, the relentless attacks, and the toll it took on the whistle-blower's life—Sarah couldn't forget the scars it left on the organization.

The wounds were still fresh, and the memories were hauntingly vivid.

But then here was Emma, with a mountain of evidence that could expose the dark underbelly of GenED's operations.

The integrity of the information was unquestionable.

Sarah thought back to GlobalPost's vow to never go down that perilous path again. They had learned their lesson; they had paid a heavy price.

But was Emma's cause worth it?

Was it worth risking everything once more?

Sarah felt a gush of emotions in her core as she reflected on the potential harm that could befall both the animals and the unwitting humans. Emma's data also hinted at a more sinister truth: an element of bio-warfare that threatened public safety and security. The implications of such nefarious activities sent shivers down Sarah's spine, for the tentacles could extend far beyond what anyone could fathom.

A battle waged within Sarah's mind—the fear of history repeating itself versus the burning desire to do what was right. She knew that publishing Emma's account would undoubtedly put them all at risk, inviting the wrath of powerful entities.

Fear engulfed her in a vice-like grip, cautioning her against provoking adversaries who could potentially bring harm to her loved ones. It urged her to step back, to protect what she held dear, and to maintain the semblance of normalcy they enjoyed.

Her thoughts were interrupted by a call on her mobile phone. It was Emily.

Sarah: Hi, sweetheart!

Emily: Mommy, Guess what? I have dance class today!

Sarah: Oh, that's wonderful, Emily! I'm so excited for you. Which dance are you learning today?

Emily: We're learning ballet! Miss Chloé said we'd be practicing our pliés and twirls.

Sarah: That sounds fantastic, sweetheart. I can't wait to see you dance. Mommy is really proud of you.

Emily: Are you coming to pick me up today? I love it when you come to watch me dance.

Sarah: Of course, Emily. I wouldn't miss it for the world. I'll be there right on time. And I love watching you, my little ballerina. You bring so much joy to my heart.

Emily: Mommy, promise me you won't be late, okay?

Sarah: I promise, sweetheart.

Emily: Mommy. I love you so much!

Sarah: I love you, Emily. You're my sunshine. Now go and have a fantastic day at school. I'll see you soon. Bye!

The call ended, leaving Sarah with a heart brimming with love.

And, as though in a flash, she had absolute clarity about what she needed to do.

She needed to protect her family and the world they lived in. Her daughter's innocent voice reminded her of what truly mattered—the safety and happiness of not only her own but the countless lives that would be affected if she faltered.

Inhaling a deep breath, Sarah smiled.

She had finally found the strength to make a difference, not just for her daughter but for all the children who deserved a safer and brighter future.

She couldn't let fear dictate her choices. She couldn't let the scars of the past paralyse her. Emma had entrusted GlobalPost with her truth, and it was their duty to give it a voice—a voice that could spark change, ignite a movement, and protect countless lives.

She reminded herself that this time would be different. They had learned from their mistakes.

They would take every precaution to protect Emma and themselves. She requested James, the legal head, to join her urgently.

Sarah: Hello James, I'm glad you're here. There's something important we need to discuss.

James: Sure thing, Sarah. I know this is serious. I have gone through the files you sent. Clearly, safety should be our top priority.

Sarah: Absolutely. We're dealing with some powerful people, and we can't afford to take any risks.

James: I understand. Our focus should be on keeping our sources and ourselves safe.

Sarah: That's exactly right. We need secure communication and file protection to ensure nothing harmful gets out.

James: Agreed. I've already started setting up a secure digital system for our investigation. And we should plan for any emergencies that might arise.

Sarah: Great idea, James. Having a backup plan is critical, and we should also have trusted allies we can count on for support in case things get out of hand.

James: I'll get right on it. Plus, we should get in touch with lawyers who specialize in protecting whistle-blowers. They can guide us through any legal challenges.

Sarah: Great idea, James.

James: And Sarah, please remember that since you are leading this, your safety is crucial. If you ever feel uneasy or unsafe, let me or our security team know immediately.

Sarah: Thanks, James. I'll be careful. Let's do this. We need to find the truth and not back down.

Over the next few tense days, Sarah and her dedicated team laboured assiduously as they verified every detail and fact-checked each piece of evidence Emma had provided. Their reputation and credibility were at stake, leaving no room for errors or oversights.

For days, Emma had been teetering on the edge of despair, tormented by Sarah's silence.

Was this all for naught?

As she stared at the blank screen, contemplating whether to log in or walk away, a voice in her mind urged her to take one last chance. Summoning every ounce of willpower, she entered her anonymous account credentials.

Right then, like lightning breaking through a dark storm, she spotted it—a single unread email from Sarah.

Subject: Re: Exposing the Truth

Dear Emma,

I hope this email finds you well. I wanted to reach out to you directly to express my utmost interest, concern, and determination to expose the truth.

First and foremost, I want to assure you that we value your safety above all else. Your identity will be protected throughout this entire process, and we will take every necessary precaution to keep you out of harm's way. Your bravery and willingness to come forward are greatly appreciated.

I wanted to inform you that the story will be published tomorrow morning, and it's crucial for you to maintain a casual demeanour and avoid any suspicion from your co-workers. We don't want to give anyone a reason to suspect your involvement or raise any red flags that could jeopardize our efforts.

Please be cautious and mindful of your interactions. Stick to your routine and avoid discussing anything related to the investigation with anyone, even those you trust implicitly. We must remain vigilant until the truth is exposed.

If you encounter any concerning or unusual situations, do not hesitate to reach out to me immediately. Please know that your safety is our top priority, and we will provide you with the necessary support and guidance throughout this process.

Thank you again for your courage. Stay strong, Emma, and know that you are not alone in this fight.

This email will self-destruct in 30 seconds after you read it.

Best regards,

Sarah Anderson

Chapter 17

Trace Me, IF You Can

As the clock struck midnight, GenED lab was shrouded in an eerie silence. Dr. Victoria was in the final stages of winding up her day. The lab hummed with the soft buzz of machinery and the lingering scent of scientific experiments.

It was at this precise instant that an urgent ping from the Cloning Confederate disrupted the tranquillity.

Dr. Victoria, sensing the gravity of the situation, urgently made her way to her concealed Video Pod, next to the Cloning Chamber.

Entering the Pod, Dr. Victoria felt a sense of heightened alertness. The reflective walls closed in around her, enclosing her in a cocoon of secrecy and protection.

With practiced hands, she typed in the encrypted access codes, her fingers dancing across the keyboard with precision.

As the video connection got established, the screen flickered to life, revealing the figures of the Cloning Confederate members.

Their identities concealed by shadow and distortion, their voices low and commanding, they wasted no time in getting to the heart of the matter. Dr. Victoria, her face projected onto the screen, listened intently, her mind sharp and focused.

Cloning Confederate: Dr. Victoria, we have received some concerning rumours regarding your involvement with a company called GenED. We suspect that there might be a damaging exposé in the media soon. Can you explain this?

Dr. Victoria: (feigning surprise) GenED? I assure you, I am not involved with any such company. Never heard of them. These rumours must be baseless speculation. I am fully committed to our cause within the Cloning Confederate.

Cloning Confederate: (sounding sceptical) We have our sources, Dr. Victoria. The information seems quite reliable. Are you absolutely certain that you have no association with GenED?

Dr. Victoria: (in a defensive tone) I swear on my dedication to the Cloning Confederate, I have no ties with GenED. I am solely focused on our research and advancing our agenda. These allegations are unfounded.

Cloning Confederate: Dr. Victoria, let us be clear. If these rumours turn out to be true and you have been deceiving us, then be prepared for the repercussions. The Cloning Confederate cannot afford to have any leaks or compromised individuals sabotaging our operations. We protect our interests at any cost.

Dr. Victoria: (speaking firmly) I assure you, there is a misunderstanding here. I am fully committed to our cause, and any allegations against me regarding GenED are false. I will cooperate in any investigation to prove my innocence.

Cloning Confederate: (in a severe tone) Dr. Victoria, we will conduct our own investigation, and if it reveals any evidence of your involvement with GenED, you will face dire consequences. Remember, the Cloning Confederate does not tolerate betrayal.

Dr. Victoria: (in a firm tone) I have dedicated my life to the Cloning Confederate and its goals. I stand by my loyalty, and I am ready to prove it beyond any doubt. I am confident that your investigation will exonerate me. I will continue to serve our cause with unswerving commitment.

And with that, the video screen flickered off.

With an impending sense of doom, Dr. Victoria immediately turned to her trusted reflection.

Dr. Victoria: Oh no, they suspect my involvement with GenED! This could unravel everything. What am I going to do?

Reflection: (Sinister tone) Calm yourself, Victoria. You mustn't let fear cloud your judgment. Remember, you are in control. They can't touch you.

Dr. Victoria: But they warned of "dire consequences", and their investigations could expose me. I can't afford to have my plans disrupted. I need to take immediate action.

Reflection: Eliminate any traces that could lead back to you. Destroy all genetic material and erase any incriminating files. Leave no evidence behind.

Dr. Victoria: You are right. I'll gather everything and send it straight to the incinerator. No one will ever find a trace of my involvement with GenED.

Reflection: Excellent. Stay focused and execute your plan flawlessly. Remember, you are cunning and resourceful. You have the power to control your destiny.

Dr. Victoria: And they will soon realise that challenging me was their gravest mistake. Beware, for crossing me will lead to deep regrets. I am unstoppable.

Reflection: That's the spirit, Victoria! You are the master of manipulation and the architect of your own fate. Stay one step ahead, and let no one obstruct your path to dominance.

Dr. Victoria emerged from the Video Pod with absolute clarity on her next steps. She immediately summoned the lab technician and her secretary, her servile and docile underlings.

Dr. Victoria: Lisa, Mark, I need your immediate assistance. Gather all the vials of genetic material from the lab and empty them into the bio-waste bins. We can't leave any trace behind.

Lisa: (in a nervous tone) Are you sure about this, Dr. Victoria? Destroying all the genetic material feels extreme.

Dr. Victoria: There's no room for hesitation, Lisa. Do as I say. Every vial must be emptied into the bio-waste bins. Mark, make sure to collect all the files and data related to our operations. We can't leave any evidence behind.

Mark: Understood, Dr. Victoria. I'll collect everything and pack it securely in a box.

Dr. Victoria: Once you have everything ready, take the box of files to the incinerator and burn them. Pay off the personnel there if you have to. We can't afford any loose ends.

Lisa: (in an anxious tone) What if someone notices the sudden disposal and becomes suspicious?

Dr. Victoria: We've planned for that, Lisa. We'll make it look like a routine disposal of expired materials. Just follow my instructions, and we'll eliminate any trace of our involvement with GenED.

Mark: Consider it done, Dr. Victoria. We'll handle the disposal discreetly and ensure that everything is completely eradicated.

Dr. Victoria: Excellent. Your loyalty and efficiency are crucial during this critical time. Remember, the success of our operation depends on our ability to cover our tracks. Now go and take care of it. Lisa, just summon the team and make sure that they all report to the lab at 6am. And yes, I want Malcolm here at 7am. Understood?

Lisa: Yes, Dr. Victoria. Understood. Shall be done.

Chapter 18

The Vanishing Act

Emma was woken up by the incessant ringing of her mobile phone, with Lisa's name flashing on the screen. Still disoriented, she stretched to grab the phone with a sense of panic in the pit of her stomach.

Lisa hissed in a stern tone." Emma, it's Lisa. I need you to report to the lab at 6 am sharp. Bring your laptop and all the data files you have in your possession. This is urgent."

Emma: Lisa, it's the middle of the night. What's going on? Is something wrong?

Lisa sounded impatient: "There's no time to explain now, Emma. Just do as I say. Bring everything you have, and make sure you're discreet. You will get to know the details once you're at the lab."

Emma gulped nervously. "Alright, Lisa. I'll be there at 6 am with everything you've asked for. But please, give me some idea of what's happening. I'm feeling quite anxious right now."

Lisa: I wish I could, Emma. Just know that we're facing a critical situation and that we need to act fast. The safety of everyone involved is at stake. See you at 6 am.

Emma quavered and muttered, "Okay, Lisa. I'll be there."

Emma felt a wave of nervousness and worry crash over her. Could she have been exposed? Was her involvement in the investigation at risk of being uncovered?

In an attempt to ease her growing anxiety, Emma quickly checked the GlobalPost website. To her relief, there was no sign of the incriminating story. Sarah's advice echoed in her mind—stay casual and continue reporting to work as if nothing had changed. But deep down, she couldn't rid herself of the nagging feeling that danger lurked around the corner.

Her hands tremoring, Emma logged onto her laptop and composed one last email to Sarah. She informed her about the urgent summons from the lab and the need for abundant caution. She emphasized the importance of staying safe and maintaining their cover. Once the email was sent, Emma speedily deleted her anonymous account, erasing any trace of their correspondence.

She nervously began copying all the evidence and files onto an encrypted hard drive.

Each click of the mouse felt like a ticking time bomb, amplifying her anxiety. Once the transfer was complete, Emma carefully concealed the drive in her secret hiding place. And then dashed off towards the lab.

As Emma stepped into the lab, she was shocked to see the transformation around her. It felt as if the entire place had been scrubbed clean, erasing any traces of its previous operations. She quickened her pace, her footsteps echoing through the emptiness as she made her way towards the conference room. The door stood slightly ajar. Emma tentatively pushed the door open and stepped into the dimly lit room. To her surprise, the conference room mirrored the rest of the lab—pristine and devoid of any indication that it had ever been occupied. The whiteboard, once filled with intricate diagrams and notes, now stood blank and immaculate. The long table, where discussions and debates had once taken place, was empty and devoid of any lingering presence.

It was as if a cleverly planned vanishing act had taken place, leaving behind only the hollow shell of a once-active laboratory.

Dr. Victoria, standing in the centre of the room, loomed large.

Her presence was commanding and intimidating, as if she had materialized out of thin air.

Dr. Victoria's probing gaze locked onto each team member who entered the room, her eyes filled with intensity. Her presence alone seemed to fill the space, casting a shadow that stretched across the room, subsuming everyone in its weight.

The team members instinctively straightened their postures, their confidence wavering under her scrutinizing gaze. They knew that whatever awaited them in this room, Dr. Victoria held the reins, and they would have to navigate this encounter with caution.

"There has been a breach," Dr. Victoria began, her voice firm and unyielding. "Our operations have been compromised, and it is imperative that we take immediate action to protect ourselves and our work."

She continued, her eyes scanning the room, making sure that every team member was listening attentively. "Effective immediately, we will disband all ongoing operations. This means ceasing all experiments, research, and any related activities. We cannot afford to take any risks at this crucial juncture. Lisa will be in charge of collecting all data, research materials, and any relevant documentation. Hand over everything you have without delay. This includes laptops, hard drives, and any other storage devices."

Her voice carried a warning tone as she emphasized, "Furthermore, all computers within this facility are to be formatted to ensure no traces of our work remain. We cannot afford any remnants that could be used against us."

"Emma," Dr. Victoria's voice, flushed with an undercurrent of distrust, cut through the silence. "You've been with us for quite some time now, working closely on this research. Yet this leak seems to have originated within our own ranks. Can you shed any light on how this could have happened?"

Emma cringed but quickly regained her composure. "I assure you, Dr. Victoria, we followed all the security protocols stringently," Emma added, continuing her charade. "I am totally shocked and deeply concerned as to how it could have happened. Are you sure there is a leak?"

Dr. Victoria's eyes narrowed, studying Emma intently for any signs of deception. Her gaze remained fixed on Emma, the suspicion still lingering in her eyes. The tension in the room was palpable as the other team members watched the exchange, their own apprehension evident.

"Anyway, for now, we must focus on conducting an internal investigation to ascertain the origin of the leak," Dr. Victoria declared, her tone having a ring of finality. "Rest assured, we will get to the bottom of this, and those responsible will be exposed. Our commitment to excellence and ethical practices will prevail."

Dr. Victoria's expression hardened as she issued a grave warning. "I want to make it explicitly clear that no member of this team is to speak to the media or divulge any information regarding our operations. Any breach of confidentiality will result in severe repercussions, both professionally and personally. We will not hesitate to take decisive action against those who betray our trust."

The room fell into an uneasy silence. With a stern gaze, she concluded, "Stay vigilant, stay loyal, and above all, protect our interests at all costs."

As the team members dispersed to carry out their assigned tasks, a tense atmosphere lingered in the room.

Each one of them grasped the gravity of their situation and the burden of hidden truths. As operations stood on the brink of collapse, confusion loomed large, and the chilling warning to remain silent reverberated in their minds. They grappled with the uncertainty of what their lives would look like in this new era of insecurity.

Chapter 19

This One is for You

At 7am, Malcolm walked into the GenED conference room, looking confused and irritated.

Malcolm: Dr. Victoria, quite frankly, I am getting really tired of your urgent summons.

Dr. Victoria: Calm down, Malcolm. We have a crisis at hand. There has been a leak, and we need to act briskly to protect ourselves.

Malcolm: What? How did this happen? Are you sure? You were running GenED like a fortress, so I am really shocked to hear this.

Dr. Victoria: Malcolm, be rest assured, if I go down, I'm taking everyone with me. That includes you. So, listen carefully and do exactly as I say. I want you to know that I've erased all evidence of GenED's operations; all genetic material is dumped in bio-waste bins. The lab is clean, and there's no trace of our research. But there's one thing left—the calf.

Malcolm: The calf? What do you mean?

Dr. Victoria: We need to put it to rest, just as we did with the surrogate. We can't leave any loose ends. I want you to ensure that the bio-waste bins and the calf are secretly disposed of without raising any suspicions. Ensure that no one ever retrieves or reconstructs the scope of our operations.

Malcolm hesitated for a brief moment, then, standing up sharply, looked Dr. Victoria in the eye. And calmly said, "No, Dr. Victoria! I cannot go along with this plan. I won't be a part of killing an innocent animal."

Dr. Victoria stood there transfixed, stunned by Malcolm's unexpected defiance. She softened her tone to make some headway. "Malcolm, you must understand the consequences if we don't eliminate all evidence. It's a necessary sacrifice to protect ourselves."

Malcolm: I don't care about the consequences anymore. This has gone too far.

Dr. Victoria: You're jeopardizing everything we've worked for, Malcolm. Are you willing to throw it all away? You're being naive, Malcolm. We're in too deep now.

Malcolm: Maybe we are, but I refuse to go down this path anymore.

Dr. Victoria: You're making a grave mistake, Malcolm. You'll regret this decision.

Malcolm: Maybe I will, but I won't let you dictate my choices anymore. I am prepared to face all eventualities, whatever they may be. Dr. Victoria, listen to me carefully. If any harm comes to that calf, I will not hesitate to expose GenED and reveal everything we've done. But if you spare the life of the calf, I will keep my silence and take the fall for our actions.

Dr. Victoria: Malcolm, you don't understand the gravity of the situation. It's not as simple as sparing one life.

Malcolm: No, you don't understand, Dr. Victoria. We've crossed lines that can never be uncrossed. I can't be a part of this any longer.

Dr. Victoria: Are you ready to risk everything, Malcolm? Your career, your reputation?

Malcolm: I'll face whatever comes my way, but I won't let another innocent life be sacrificed. We have a choice here, Dr. Victoria, to change the narrative and to take responsibility for our actions.

Dr. Victoria: You're asking me to choose between my life's work and the life of a calf?

Malcolm: I'm asking you to choose between perpetuating a cycle of harm and finding a way to make amends. You have my word. I will take the fall. I will deny your involvement. I will publicly claim that GenED is totally my doing. As you have already erased all evidence, I will open the gates for any possible investigations. They will not find any proof here. Eventually, I will disband NectarMeadow. In exchange, you will spare the life of the calf. Do we have a deal?

Dr. Victoria fumed with indignation. "Fine, Malcolm. Spare the calf. But know that this decision is a fatal mistake, and it will come back to haunt you." And with that, Dr. Victoria stormed out of the conference room.

With a sense of urgency, Malcolm hurried out of the conference room, his mind a whirlwind of thoughts. There was so much to be done and so many pieces to set in motion.

But first and foremost, he needed to call Aster. He planned to reinstate Aster and entrust the care of the calf to his capable and dedicated hands.

As Emma cleaned up her desk, every minute felt like an eternity. She waited with bated breath for the story to break. In her mind, she played out various scenarios, planning how she would navigate the aftermath and deal with Dr. Victoria once the truth was exposed.

As the seconds ticked by, her phone suddenly beeped. It was the notification she had been waiting for.

With unsteady hands, Emma clicked on the article titled "Say No to GMO Milk: Unmasking the Horrors of GenED's Operations."

And right in the centre was the image of c-Luna in the birthing chamber. The story painted a vivid and damning portrait of GenED's operations.

Tears of relief cascaded down Emma's face, tracing a path of both anguish and triumph. In that moment, the burden of her relentless pursuit of the truth lifted, allowing an avalanche of emotions to inundate her being.

Each droplet of emotion that rolled down her cheeks felt like a betrayal of the façade she had crafted.

Breathing deeply, Emma composed herself, reminding herself of the cameras that acutely mapped all her moves.

It was essential that she play her part convincingly for the next stage of her plan, creating an illusion of surprise and innocence.

Emma wiped away the tears and whispered under her breath "This one is for you, Fred".

As she fortified her spirit, Emma steeled herself for the intricate dance of deception that awaited.

Emma rushed to inform Dr. Victoria about the breaking news, portraying a sense of utter shock. She wanted to catch Dr. Victoria off guard, capitalizing on the element of surprise. As she approached Dr. Victoria's office, she took a deep breath, preparing herself to put on the 'performance' of her life.

Emma burst into the office, her face flushed and her voice shaky. "Dr. Victoria," she stammered, her voice filled with apparent distress. "You won't believe what just happened. There's a news story... it's about GenED and the cloning operations. It's everywhere!"

Dr. Victoria, taken aback by Emma's sudden appearance and agitated state, looked up from her desk, her expression laced with curiosity. "What? What are you talking about?" she asked, her voice betraying a hint of panic.

"It's all over the internet," Emma continued, her voice quivering. "They're exposing everything— our practices, the apparent mistreatment of animals, the human health risks. It's a disaster!"

Emma continued, feigning confusion and helplessness. "It's spreading like wildfire. We need to do damage control and figure out how to respond. We can't let this ruin our work."

After what felt like an interminably long stunned silence, Dr. Victoria finally responded, her voice laced with fear and frustration: "We need to get a crisis management team ready. We need to act fast and control the narrative. We can't let them bring us down."

Emma nodded in agreement, internally rejoicing that her plan to outmanoeuvre Dr. Victoria seemed to have worked.

Chapter 20

Catching the Wave

"Say No to GMO Milk" broke the internet with explosive force, igniting a wave of public outrage. Within minutes of the release of the story, social media platforms were ablaze with hashtags like #SayNotoGMOMilk, #Freec-Luna, and #SaveSurrogates, capturing the attention of millions. The story's shocking content, backed by compelling evidence, struck a chord with the public, galvanising their emotions and igniting a strong demand for transparency and meaningful change.

The image of c-Luna in the birthing chamber provoked intense emotions in people around the world. c-Luna metamorphosed into a powerful symbol of resilience, compassion, and the battle against unethical practices. It captured hearts across the globe, uniting people from all walks of life under a single heartfelt rallying cry.

As the hashtags gained traction, they became trending topics, rapidly spreading across online platforms.

Users shared the story, expressed their outrage, and demanded action against GenED and those involved.

Celebrities, activists, and influencers joined the conversation, amplifying the message and lending their support to the cause.

The public outcry and viral nature of the story created a domino effect. News outlets and media organizations picked up on the story, shining an even brighter spotlight on GenED and its questionable practices. The issue resonated with varied groups, from animal rights activists to health-conscious consumers, prompting debates and discussions on the ethics of genetically modified food and the mistreatment of animals in the agricultural industry.

As news of the exposé spread like wildfire, activist groups rallied together in a powerful display of solidarity and passion. They organized protests and demonstrations outside the gates of NectarMeadow, their voices echoed in unison. The air was filled with chants, signs, and impassioned speeches.

Journalists from various news outlets and television stations lined up, eager to capture the stories and sentiments of those demanding justice for the animals and advocating for food safety. Microphones were thrust towards activists and protestors, who passionately expressed their concerns.

Activist 1: "We gather here not only to advocate for the rights of animals but also to shed light on the potential health risks associated with genetically modified food. We must not overlook the impact that these practices can have on human well-being."

Activist 2: "We have seen the haunting image of c-Luna, trapped in a world that denies her the right to live free and experience the natural joys of life. It is our duty to speak up for them, to be their voice, and to fight for their rights."

Activist 3: "Genetically modified organisms have inundated our food system, silently infiltrating our diets without our knowledge. We urge the public to exercise caution and demand proper labelling of genetically modified products. It is our right to make informed decisions about what we consume and feed our families."

Activist 4: "We gather here united by a common cause—to fight for the voiceless, the innocent, who suffer behind the walls of NectarMeadow. We must demand transparency and justice for the animals who have endured unimaginable pain and cruelty."

Activist 5: "Let us not be swayed by false promises of convenience and abundance, but rather prioritize our health and the health of future generations. Today, we stand united in our call for transparent and rigorous testing of genetically modified food, including milk produced by cloned cows."

As Malcolm watched the sea of protestors from his office window, their passionate voices resonated deep within his soul. With a bleeding heart, he made his way towards the gates, ready to confront the protestors and the swarming media. As he stepped into the midst of the crowd, a hush fell over the assembly, all eyes fixed on him. He climbed atop a makeshift podium as swarms of journalists shoved microphones and cameras in his face.

As he began speaking, a lull fell over the assembly.

"I stand before you with a heavy heart and a deep sense of remorse. It is with the utmost humility that I address the misunderstandings and misguided beliefs that have caused the suffering of innocent animals and created potential risks to human health. I express my deepest regret for the pain inflicted upon these animals and the misplaced trust that was driven by the relentless pursuit of profit."

"I am happy to share with you that c-Luna has been freed from the confines of the lab."

"She now roams the pastures, her rightful place, experiencing the freedom and peace that were unjustly denied to her for far too long."

"In light of the grave aftermath and the lessons learned, I declare that all experiments conducted at NectarMeadow will be immediately disbanded. We will cease our operations without hesitation. It is time for a profound change, a transformation that begins with acknowledging the mistakes of our past.

With a heavy heart, I accept full responsibility for the excesses that have occurred under my watch. I understand that what transpired was a direct result of my decisions and actions. Today, I stand before you, humbled and ready to face the consequences of my actions. I am committed to making amends for the harm caused to the trust of the public.

Our journey towards redemption and restoration will not be an easy one. I pledge to work closely with animal rights organizations, experts, and regulatory bodies to ensure that the safety and well-being of animals are prioritized. We will rebuild the shattered trust, brick by brick, as we embark on a new path.

To those who remain sceptical, I understand your concerns. My words alone are not enough, and I recognize the need for tangible actions to accompany them."

"I urge you to hold me accountable, as I hold myself accountable, for the promises made here today. Let us work together, hand in hand, to create a future where the well-being of animals is safeguarded, potential risks to human health are minimized, and where compassion and empathy guide our every action.

Thank you. May we find solace in the pursuit of a better tomorrow."

Getting off the podium, Malcolm made his way back to his office, his heart filled with a sense of relief and liberation. As he walked, each step carried him further away from the burden of the past.

As he entered his office, Malcolm closed the door behind him, shutting out the noise and commotion of the outside world. The silence enveloped him, and he leaned against his desk to let the emotions wash over him. He looked out of the window, his gaze fixed on the horizon, the world seemed to stretch before him, brimming with possibilities. He rolled up his sleeves, eager for a fresh start, free from the shackles of the past.

Dr. Victoria sat glued to the live feed of the happenings at the NectarMeadow gate.

As she watched Malcolm take the fall, she heaved a sigh of relief.

With him shouldering the blame, she was now in the clear and seemed to have escaped any major repercussions.

An urgent notification flashed on her screen, indicating a crucial message from the Cloning Confederate. In a flash, she made her way to her Video Pod, and started the video call. As the connection was established, a masked figure appeared on the screen, their voice distorted to protect their identity.

"Dr. Victoria, you have handled this crisis well," the masked figure commended, their tone laced with satisfaction and caution. "To ensure your safety and the integrity of our operations, we advise you to go underground until the storm subsides."

The masked figure continued, their words measured and deliberate. "Send us all the research data, files, and any remaining evidence you possess. We will analyse it thoroughly. We will leave no stone unturned to uncover the traitor within our ranks responsible for the leak," the masked figure assured, their voice taking on an ominous tone. "Their betrayal will not go unpunished; they shall face our wrath."

With a final warning to maintain her secrecy and vigilance, the video call ended.

Dr. Victoria stared at her multi-layered reflection in the mirror, her eyes burning with rage.

Dr. Victoria: This is not over. Not by a long shot. I will gather my resources, regroup, and come back.

Reflection: They think they've won, don't they? But they have no idea what you are capable of, Victoria. The traitor will pay a heavy price for their betrayal.

Dr. Victoria: They may have temporarily gained the upper hand, but they underestimate my resilience. I will not be defeated.

Reflection: Victoria, we've faced setbacks before, but we've always risen above them. This time will be no different. We will rebuild and strike back with full force.

Dr. Victoria: With you by my side, anything and everything is possible. We will emerge from the shadows stronger and more formidable than ever. This is just the beginning.

Chapter 21

The Bold Promise

As the gentle sun of a brand new day lit the room, Emma slowly opened her eyes. A smile blossomed on her face, the reflection of a heart filled with renewed hope and purpose.

It had been nearly a month since the grand exposé, but the public's imagination was still captivated by the story.

The internet and news channels buzzed with the emotionally stirring voices of the protagonists of the public movement that had rallied together to rescue c-Luna, the symbol of hope and resilience amidst a sinister operation.

The aftermath was a flurry of divided opinions and heated debates surrounding Malcolm's actions. Was he truly a hero, a courageous figure willing to make sacrifices to save lives?

Some praised his bravery, seeing him as a champion of justice, while others sceptically probed his motives and level of involvement.

The lines between hero and antihero blurred, leaving the world to grapple with the complexity of his choices and their consequences.

In the midst of the whirling sea of opinions, one undeniable truth emerged: the power of the people had triumphed.

Emma felt an irresistible pull to visit NectarMeadow one last time and express her appreciation for Malcolm.

The courage he had shown and the sacrifice he had made to protect c-Luna, had left a lasting impression on her. As she approached the familiar gates, she felt a forceful and profound sense of connection to the place that held the stories of both suffering and redemption.

Malcolm sat at his desk, surrounded by a chaotic sprawl of blueprints and sketches. His desk resembled a battlefield, with a patchwork of intricate plans, crisscrossing lines, and elaborately drawn diagrams. The blueprints bore the marks of countless revisions and hastily jotted notes.

Lost in his thoughts, Malcolm didn't notice the sound of the door opening as Emma quietly entered the room.

She took a step closer, careful not to disturb the reverie that held him captive. A soft smile tugged at the corner of Emma's lips as she said, "Hello Malcolm, nice to meet you."

Malcolm, startled, looked up. "Emma! I'm sorry; I didn't notice you coming in. Please have a seat."

Emma: (taking a seat) No need to apologize, Malcolm. It's inspiring to see how immersed you are in your vision. I came by because I wanted to thank you for what you did for c-Luna. You showed incredible courage to stand up for her and all the innocent animals at NectarMeadow.

Malcolm: (with a gentle smile) You don't have to thank me. I regret not doing it sooner.

Malcolm hesitated, searching for the right words, and then continued. "Emma, there is something I wanted to share with you. Aster told me about your efforts to save Shanti, and I want you to know how deeply thankful I am."

Emma: (taken aback) Oh, I didn't realize Aster had mentioned it to you. Yes, I did everything I could to protect Shanti, but I failed. I am so sorry. It broke my heart to see Shanti go.

Malcolm: Don't be sorry, Emma; let's find comfort in knowing that we did all that we could. Now it's time to work towards a brilliant future that overshadows all the pains of the past.

Malcolm leaned forward as he looked deeply into Emma's eyes.

"These blueprints and maps represent the culmination of countless hours of brainstorming and refining. I believe I have hit upon the perfect plan to resurrect NectarMeadow and bring about a miraculous transformation. Would you like to know more?"

With curiosity and excitement in her eyes, Emma exclaimed "Absolutely, tell me more!"

Malcolm: (spreading out a large sheet) Take a look at this sketch. It's the concept for a magical theme park called c-Luna Farm.

Malcolm continued with an excited smile. "Since c-Luna has captured my heart and the hearts of millions, it's only fitting that she be our mascot."

Emma: (gazing at the sketch with wonder) Amazing, Malcolm! This looks incredible. A theme park centred around c-Luna and promoting animal-human connection. I love the concept.

Malcolm: Absolutely, Emma. The park will feature a Healing Centre where visitors can spend intimate time with cows. Research has shown that such interactions release oxytocin, relieving anxiety and stress. It's also proven to be therapeutic for individuals with severe mental disorders.

Emma: That's fascinating! Providing a space for people to connect with cows on a deeper level can truly have a positive impact on their well-being. I can already imagine the healing and calming effect it can bring.

Malcolm: Exactly. In addition to the Healing Centre, we'll have Play and Recreation zone with cow-shaped thrillrides and a nature park.

An Art Centre, where stories of animal-human connection and cooperation will be showcased, and a range of c-Luna merchandise like stuffed toys, t-shirts, mugs, and comic books.

Emma: That sounds delightful! The Nature Park with its joyrides and the Art Centre will undoubtedly create a memorable and enriching experience for visitors, and the merchandise will allow them to take a piece of c-Luna's magic home with them.

Malcolm: (pointing out to the north side of the design) This will be the Production Centre. We'll be producing cow-free and plant-based milk here and exporting it worldwide.

And that's not all. (pointing out the south section of the chart) Here we will have a Science and Innovation Centre dedicated to finding solutions to boost immunity and longevity in farmed animals. It's our commitment to advancing animal welfare and ensuring their well-being so that they are treated as sentient beings and not mere production units.

Emma: That's remarkable, Malcolm. It's amazing to see the breadth and depth of your vision for c-Luna Farm. I'm truly inspired by this initiative.

Malcolm: So then, are you with me, Emma? I would like you to join me as a partner to make this vision a reality.

Emma: (taken aback, her eyes welling up with emotions) Malcolm, I... I don't know what to say. This is so unexpected, and I'm overwhelmed.

After a few brief moments, Emma began to speak slowly. "I believe in the future we can create together. A future where everyone, humans and animals alike, can thrive and find their place in this interconnected web of life. My answer is 'yes', a thousand times 'yes'!"

Emma hesitated a bit as she continued. "There is one favour I'd like to ask, Malcolm. It would mean a lot to me. Could we name the Science and Innovation Centre after Fred Astridge? He believed in our cause, and this would be a fitting tribute to his memory."

Malcolm: (smiling broadly) That is a beautiful idea. I understand how much Fred meant to you, and it would be an honour to have the Science and Innovation Centre named after him. Consider it done.

Emma: Thank you, Malcolm; I am deeply touched.

Just then Malcolm's phone pinged.

Malcolm: This is unbelievable, Emma! You are my lucky charm! WildFrontier Funders have just confirmed that they will invest in c-Luna Farm! Although it's a small amount, it's a great start to regain my credibility in the industry. Let's get started!

Over the next few months, Emma and Malcolm became an unstoppable force, working day and night to turn their shared dream into a tangible reality.

Every decision they made was infused with intention and purpose, as what they sought to create was not just a project but a legacy.

And finally, the day they had been praying for, working for, and hoping for arrived—the grand opening of c-Luna Farm to the public.

Malcolm and Emma stood at the entrance, their hearts overflowing with pride as they witnessed the sea of people thronging to enter. The once-tainted gates of NectarMeadow stood reborn, now a symbol of hope and transformation, drawing crowds from all around the world.

The NectarMeadow farm had magically transformed into c-Luna Farm, a grand spectacle and a place where dreams and possibilities converged.

The air buzzed with energy and the contagious enthusiasm of the crowd.

The visitors revelled in the enchanting ambiance of the Nature Park as they strolled through lush green pathways, surrounded by a symphony of birdsong and the soothing rustle of leaves.

Spotting c-Luna and her herd became an exhilarating experience for the children, filling them with joy and wonder as they marvelled at the majestic creatures grazing in the distance.

The scent of wildflowers and fresh earth filled the air, providing a sense of tranquillity and harmony with nature.

Families gathered around crystal-clear ponds, watching graceful swans gliding across the water, while others took leisurely boat rides, mesmerised by the reflections of the vibrant landscape. The Nature Park's diverse attractions, from thrilling cow-shaped joyrides to serene meditation spots, catered to every taste, leaving the visitors captivated and engaged.

The multi-award-winning documentary on Cow Cuddling Therapy, showcasing its global impact, was screened at the Arts Centre. The audience gave it a standing ovation, sparking conversations about cows' role in managing mental and emotional health issues in humans.

The c-Luna merchandise held a unique power, like a talisman, that resonated with people on a profound level. It became a symbol of hope, connection, and a shared mission.

For many, owning c-Luna merchandise was like possessing a piece of magic—a tangible reminder of the extraordinary story and the journey of triumph over adversity.

At the heart of it all, the Healing Centre provided a sanctuary for those seeking support and connection.

Visitors experienced the therapeutic effects of spending intimate time with cows and finding relief from anxiety and stress. Beyond its restorative qualities, the Healing Centre also extended its reach to those with severe mental disorders. It offered a safe space, free from judgement, where individuals could find guidance and therapy.

The presence of the cows, with their innate ability to sense and respond to emotions, provided an environment that nurtured emotional and mental well-being.

Meanwhile, Fred Astridge Science and Innovation Centre, was a hub for research and progress. Dedicated scientists worked diligently to find solutions to the most pressing health challenges faced by farm animals.

The cow-free alternative milk produced by The Precision Fermentation Division and the Plant Milk Division, found their way to the farthest corners of the world and started generating profits for c-Luna Farm.

In the midst of it all, c-Luna stood tall as the star attraction, radiating grace and resilience.

People lined up for a chance to capture a selfie with her, to be in the presence of a living symbol of hope and victory.

To them, c-Luna embodied triumph over adversity, a living testament to the indomitable spirit that shines within every living being.

The global media churned out screaming headlines.

"From Controversy to Triumph: c-Luna Farm Stuns the World with Its Vision"

"A New Era Begins: c-Luna Farm Captivates Hearts and Minds"

"c-Luna Farm Launch: A Resounding Success in Bridging the Gap Between Humans and Animals"

"A Bright Future: c-Luna Farm Promises a Paradigm Shift "

As the magical day drew to a close, Emma and Malcolm stood together, taking in the beauty of c-Luna Farm, bathed in the mesmerising warm colours of twilight.

Despite the insurmountable odds, their shared vision had become a reality, impacting millions of lives.

They knew that this was just the beginning of an extraordinary journey that awaited them.

Chapter 22

The Ticking Time Bomb

The world was irretrievably altered and endangered by Dr. Victoria's sinister experiments at NectarMeadow.

Lurking in the shadows, the Cloning Confederate had been working tirelessly to harness the data produced by these experiments, and an explosive blueprint had emerged that could tip the scales of power in their favour.

The credibility that Dr. Victoria lost in the NectarMeadow leak fiasco was eclipsed by the newfound recognition she garnered within the Confederate's inner circle due to the brilliance of the data she provided.

Her transformation from an outcast scientist to a vital player in their grand designs was complete.

No longer content with mere subterfuge, the Cloning Confederate were preparing for a move of unparalleled audacity.

This time, they vowed, there would be no room for error.

And the world would soon bear witness to the magnitude of their ambition and the depth of their ruthlessness.

ABOUT THE AUTHOR

CHANDNI JAFRI is a triple bottom-line proponent, angel investor, start-up evangelist, Founder and CEO, Advisor, theatre producer and actor.

She is the Executive Director of Jafri Foundation.The aim of Jafri Foundation is to preserve and perpetuate the legacy of Vilayet Jafri by giving a platform to underrepresented artists and art forms and performing Sound & Light shows globally.

Chandni is a graduate in Biochemistry and holds an MBA. She played Badminton at the professional circuit and was the UP State Badminton Women's Doubles & Mixed Doubles champion, 1991-1992.

Chandni practices Buddhism, numerology and is a Reiki Master.